Lee, Willis Thomas

The Face of the Earth as seen from the Air

A study in the application of airplane photography to geography

Lee, Willis Thomas

The Face of the Earth as seen from the Air

A study in the application of airplane photography to geography

Inktank publishing, 2018

www.inktank-publishing.com

ISBN/EAN: 9783750133457

THE FACE OF THE EARTH AS SEEN FROM THE AIR

A Study in the Application of Airplane Photography to Geography

BY

WILLIS T. LEE
U. S. Geological Survey

AMERICAN GEOGRAPHICAL SOCIETY
BROADWAY AT 156TH STREET
NEW YORK
1922

CONTENTS

LIST OF ILLUSTRATIONS

(o) indicates an oblique, (v) a vertical airplane photograph

SUBMERGED LAND FORMS

THE PLAIN FROM THE AIR

MOUNTAIN FEATURES

All of the airplane photographs in this book, both oblique and vertical, were taken by the United States Army Air Service, except Figs. 78 and 79, which were taken by the United States Navy Air Service, and Figs. 10, 65, 69, 75, 77, and 82, which were taken by the author. To these two services the author is indebted for the permission to reproduce their photographs, and this acknowledgment is made with the same force as if made individually under each illustration.

As a guide to the evaluation of the scale of the vertical photographs, which is expressed under each photograph in the form of the natural scale, or representative fraction, the following approximate equivalents may be borne in mind:

1:10,000 = 800 + feet to the inch
1:16,000 = ¼ mile to the inch
1:21,000 = ⅓ mile to the inch

INTRODUCTION

Scarcely a generation has passed during the evolution of the airplane from a ridiculous dream to a practical factor in the work of the world. Men who once read with derision, or only passive interest at best, of the experiments of Langley, Chanute, and the Wrights have seen the airplane developed suddenly into an indispensable instrument of war and an agency of demonstrated value and of such diversity of application that its future is hard to estimate.

The navigation of the air has accomplished much in many fields. Not only does it offer a new means of efficiency in military reconnaissance, rapid delivery of mail, fire patrol of forests, and the constantly increasing number of commercial and scientific pursuits to which it is being adapted; but it has also opened a new world to the geographer, the physiographer, and the geologist.

Airplane Photography: Its Development and Application

Very early in the war the airplane was recognized as a useful, in fact a necessary, means of observing enemy positions and movements. But the speed of the airplane was found to preclude the taking of more than the most hurried of notes during a flight, and notes written from memory are not the most satisfactory. Photography was found to obviate this difficulty. The ability of the camera to make instantaneous exposures and fix a clear image on a photographic plate enabled the observer to obtain a record not only of the scenes that he had viewed but also of many that he might have missed while engaged in the necessary business of watching the sky for the enemy—a record that for detail and accuracy could not be approached by the most elaborate notes or the most graphic description. Immediately inventive genius was set at work to adjust the mechanism of the camera to the demands of air photography and to prepare the rapidly working films and highly sensitized paper necessary for the best results.

So satisfactory were the results and so great are the possibilities of further adaptation that there is an unfortunate tendency on the part of certain enthusiasts to make exaggerated claims that may react to retard progress. This is particularly true in the use of the air photograph in mapping. There are limitations to this use of air photography. It cannot be reasonably expected to do away entirely with the ground work of the surveyor. Rather, the camera is to be regarded as one of the instruments of the surveyor. Observation from the air can never take the place of close examination of the ground, but it can be of great use in the location and study of land forms and geologic relations. Air photography is only an added means of obtaining information, although it promises to become a very important means.

Observations from the air described in numerous reports and articles in geographic magazines during the war and since its close indicate that air craft, especially in connection with air photography, can be of great use in studying the physical features of the face of the earth. In order to make a practical test of the use of the airplane in the study of geography the writer spent about nine months during the year 1920 making flights, taking pictures from air craft, and gathering information from various sources. This book embodies the chief results.

The material presented here is by way of illustrating the possibility of using the airplane and airplane photography as a means of securing information that should become increasingly useful in the study of geography, and of showing geographic and geologic features better than in any other way. The views have been chosen to illustrate the three uses of air photographs with which this book deals—the presentation of new views of subjects of popular interest and the practical value of such views; the study of land forms from a new and advantageous point of view; and the use of the air photograph as an aid in mapping.

In presenting these illustrations there is no intention that the list of types should be considered in any sense complete. Physiographic observation from the air is a relatively new undertaking, and results are limited and imperfect. As improvements in mechanism and technique are made, observations will be extended and better photographs and a greater variety of them will be secured. Such as are presented here, however, serve to demonstrate that the air photograph will come to be recognized as a valuable source of information for the student of geography and geology.

ACKNOWLEDGMENTS

The results here presented were secured by the co-operation of the Air Services of the United States Army and Navy. Hydroplanes were placed at my disposal on several occasions, and a number of flights were made over water bodies, particularly over the Potomac River, Chesapeake Bay, and New York Harbor. But the information was gathered chiefly through the Army Air Service. Many flights were made in army planes, some for general observation, others for photographing specific objects. Also the army photographers, particularly those at Langley Field, near Newport News, Va., made several photographic trips at my request, and a large number of prints were furnished from negatives stored at this and other flying fields.

In this connection I wish to express appreciation for the many courtesies extended by Major General C. T. Menoher, U. S. A., Chief of Air Service at the time the work was done, and by Major J.W. Simons, Jr., A.S., Acting Administrative Executive, Air Service. These officers placed at my disposal every facility of the service that I could use. It would be a pleasure, if space allowed, to mention the names of the numerous pilots and other officers to whom I am directly indebted for the safe completion of some of the most thrilling adventures of my life. I must, however, mention the officer to whom I am perhaps more indebted than to any other. My introduction to this study was through Major J.W. Bagley of the United States Army Engineering Corps, who has done much toward making the camera a valuable instrument in mapping.[1] Through his active interest I became acquainted with the officials of the Army Air Service, who gave the necessary authorization for flights and for securing most of the photographs used to illustrate this book. During the time spent at this work I retained my position as geologist of the United States Geological Survey. Hence the work is one of co-operation chiefly between the United States Army Air Service and the United States Geological Survey, and to a lesser degree with the United States Navy Air Service.

[1] Cf. his The Use of the Panoramic Camera in Topographic Surveying, With Notes on the Application of Photogrammetry to Aerial Surveys. *U. S. Geol. Survey Bull. 657*, Washington, D. C., 1917.

CHAPTER I

THE VIEWPOINT

(Figs. 1 to 4)

Oblique and Vertical Airplane Photographs

Air photographs are, in general, of two sorts, depending upon whether the photograph was taken with the camera pointing vertically or obliquely downward. In either case the air photographer is free from the limitations that hamper the ground photographer in choosing a point of view. For he can ascend to any desired height and not only select an advantageous position from which to photograph the feature which he wishes to emphasize but also, at the same time, avoid obstacles which might obstruct his view from the ground. Vertical photographs are preferable where the accurate location of objects is desired. When properly taken they serve many of the purposes of maps and are, in many ways, even more useful than maps. They furnish the untrained mind with much of the information that the trained mind reads from a topographic map and, in addition, supply details and relations that a map cannot depict. Exact accuracy, however, cannot be claimed for them until they have been corrected for distortion and adjusted to some system of controls.

Where the photograph is to be used as a means of securing a more advantageous view of a subject than can be had from the ground rather than as a map on which distances are to be scaled off, the oblique photograph is probably the more desirable, since it is as easily intelligible as a photograph taken laterally. The advantage of such photographs is obvious. To the architect, the landscape gardener, the city planner is given the opportunity to study their projects free from all obstructions yet in such perspective that their relations to their surroundings are brought out as would be possible by no other means. Views like that of West Point (Fig. 3) are occasionally to be had from some hilltop, but the limited choice of position on the ground contrasts sharply with the unlimited choice in the air.

Elements to Be Recorded

Air photography is by no means simple. Much still remains to be done by way of adapting the camera to its peculiar demands. Its present degree of perfection, of course, is largely due to the impetus given its development during the war because of its great importance in military reconnaissance. The adaptation of the camera to operation from the airplane might be described with profit but will be passed with slight mention because it is the results of air photography rather than the mechanism that are to be considered here. Technically, a photograph of the earth's surface may not be a map, but, given certain means of interpretation, it can be made to serve as such. In using air photographs, particularly the vertical ones, it is desirable to know the scale, which is dependent upon the altitude at which the exposure is made: the angle of the lens; and the variation from the vertical, in order to make corrections for distortion. Therefore, it is desirable that each photograph show the altitude, date, time of day, and position of the lens at which the exposure was made. Cameras have been constructed that automatically record these data on each negative. This information is illustrated in Figure 2. The circular symbol at the left in the white strip at the top of the photograph represents a circular level, or inclinometer. The small round dot close to the center of the inclinometer indicates that, at the time the exposure was made, the axis of the lens was very nearly vertical. The symbol in the center of the white strip indicates an altitude of about 9,800 feet, and that at the right, that the exposure was made 7 seconds after 11 A. M. The other symbols record that this photograph was No. 13 of a series made at Rochester, N. Y., October 23, 1920, with an Eastman mapping camera known as K–2. The symbol 8-P is non-essential and records that this negative is No. 8 of panchromatic film.

The information given by the symbols is corroborated by the

FIG. 2 Symbols of automatic register in the Eastman mapping camera, photographed with the body of the picture showing roads, streams, orchards, cultivated fields, etc. For explanation of the symbols, see the text.

picture. Orchard and shade trees appear as circular dots in place of the elongated images characteristic of pictures taken obliquely downward, and the short, squat shadows denote exposure near midday. Shocks of corn standing in the fields show that the season is autumn.

How to Read Airplane Photographs

Not all the features, however, are so easily recognizable. Oblique photographs are often more readily interpreted than ordinary photographs, since they combine with the usual view the essentials of a plan; but in vertical photographs very few objects present an appearance that is natural in the light of our experience as lateral observers. The uninitiated, on attempting systematically to identify the features of a vertical photograph, find a very large number that are foreign in appearance. A necessary preliminary is an acquaintance with the ground photographed or with similar regions and features. Without such a key the air photograph is not always self-interpretative and is often unintelligible. Military observers are carefully trained to recognize features of military significance. It is not to be expected, however, that they should be trained in the observation of land forms except such as are of military importance. Consequently, whereas a great variety of photographs is now easily obtainable at many flying fields, the information that a scientist would desire concerning them is not so easily available. Most of the photographs used in this paper were taken by men who were not trained in observing land forms. Many were taken simply as a requirement in practice flights and meant so little to the observer that no record was made concerning them. For several not even the location was recorded.

It is of primary importance that the picture be held in the right position. Not only must the observer imagine himself looking directly down on the scene but he must hold the photograph in the position in which experience has shown that the image appears the most natural. Otherwise a depression will appear as an elevation and an elevation as a hollow. It is a well-known fact that in telescopic photographs of the moon the craters appear like hollows when the print is held in one position and like elevations when the position is reversed. Experience shows that if the print is held *so that the shadows fall toward the observer* the objects appear natural. The reason is that the observer sees only those shadows that are caused by light falling towards him. Consequently, the only interpretation that the brain can give to shadows on a photograph is that they are cast by an elevation between the eye and the light. In a picture, therefore, in which shadows fall away from the eye instead of towards it valleys are seen as hills and hills as valleys. In the northern hemisphere this prescribed orientation conflicts with the convention of placing the north side of a map at the top of the page and also with the modern shaded map on which the light is represented as coming from the upper left, or northwest, corner of the map.

Failure of Air Photographs to Show Relief, and Measures to Remedy This Defect

In photographs taken from the ground the lights and shadows are such that a high degree of naturalness is possible. But objects seen from directly above, and even those viewed obliquely, though to a lesser degree, are illuminated so uniformly that photographs of them are apt to appear flat. To some extent this has been overcome by the use of extra-sensitive emulsions, special ray filters, and printing papers adapted for accentuating contrast. Many of the photographs used in this book did not allow satisfactory reproduction till the contrast of the negatives was greatly increased by the arts of the photographic laboratory. But, even at its best, no photograph taken vertically affords an adequate idea of the height of hills or the depth of hollows. Only shadows that are particularly well defined can be distinguished as shadows, while small elevations and depressions affect the negative no differently than a difference in marking or color. In military defenses, if the mere surface of the camouflage is sufficiently realistic, the ordinary camera is even more easily deceived than the human eye. It is a well-known fact that man and other animals of the higher order see objects in relief, within a certain range of vision, because the eyes convey to their respective retinas slightly different images of the same object which the brain combines into a relief image. The stereoscopic camera has long been used for the same purpose. Its principle, with certain adaptations that need not be discussed here, has been to some extent employed in airplane pictures, with such excellent results that it is claimed by some that by further development actual contouring will be possible by this means. It is reported that in military reconnaissance stereoscopic pictures render ordinary camouflage useless and that bridges, observation towers, gun emplacements, etc., are shown in relief and, therefore, easily detected.[1]

[1] H. E. Ives: Airplane Photography, Philadelphia, 1920, pp. 328–350.

CHAPTER II

FAMILIAR SCENES FROM A NEW ANGLE

(Figs. 1, 3, and 4)

Pictures of well-known buildings are of wide appeal. In so far as they create an interest in the activities for which the buildings stand they are distinctly educative. Such widely known buildings as the National Capitol and the Library of Congress are used repeatedly for illustration. They are as welcome as the sight of a familiar face. Any unusual circumstance connected with them is seized upon as an excuse for republishing pictures of them. Views of them from a new angle are always in demand. Not only do air photographs offer a welcome novelty, but they have the added advantage of lifting the subject out of the clutter of surrounding buildings and making it really the central figure of the picture. It would be difficult to get a more impressive view of the National Capitol than that of Figure 1 or a more attractive glimpse of the Naval Academy at Annapolis than that of Figure 4. The objects of chief interest occupy the center of view without distracting obstructions. In the former, the imposing structure of the Capitol building appears in a pleasing setting of minor details. The proximity of the Senate Office Building and the Library of Congress is at once apparent, and the radiating systems of the avenues of approach. Strangers may have wondered as to the nature of the environs of the Capitol. The tree-lined streets and the apartment houses seen in the picture answer the question. In the view of the Naval Academy the buildings occupy the center of the scene, with the beautiful dome of the memorial to John Paul Jones, the first great American naval fighter, prominently in view. Spa Creek in the foreground, a part of the capital city of Maryland at the left, and the Severn River, with its low wooded banks, stretching away

FIG. 4 The Naval Academy at Annapolis, Md. Oblique view from an airplane from a position over Eastport in a general northwesterly direction. The water in the foreground is Spa Creek. The Severn River, spanned by the county bridge and the Baltimore and Annapolis Railroad bridge, stretches away to the left. The buildings in the middle of the picture are those of the Naval Academy. The domed mausoleum built in honor of John Paul Jones, which serves as his final resting place, appears at the left. Still farther to the left lies Maryland's capital city. Of interest is a comparison of the low-lying and stream-cut banks of the drowned valley now occupied by the Severn River with the mountains through which the Hudson River has cut its gorge at West Point (see Fig. 3).

in the distance, spanned by the county bridge and the Baltimore and Annapolis Railroad bridge, form an interesting setting and show, without detracting from the importance of the academy itself, its advantageous location with regard to the city and the water approaches.

CHAPTER III

ARCHITECTURE, LANDSCAPE GARDENING, AND ENGINEERING

(Figs. 5 to 14)

Only a few photographs are necessary to show how valuable to the architect, the construction engineer, the city planner, or the landscape gardener the air photograph, both vertical and oblique, is destined to become. Pictorial records of progress in the construction of buildings, bridges, ships, canals, reservoirs, etc., that partake also of the nature of ground plans, as do air photographs, furnish an admirable means of study and comparison. No photograph of the great shipyards at Newport News taken from the ground would show the relation of the shops and drydocks to the deep-water approaches as does Figure 7. Figure 8 gives an unusually comprehensive idea of the location, magnitude, and construction of Hell Gate Bridge; and Figure 10, Rockaway Beach, now a densely populated town where a few years ago was a barren strip of sand, suggests that photographic records of construction in rapidly growing communities where changes are being made in streets, railroads, and buildings, will come to be a part of the equipment of the city engineer and architect.

Architecture and Landscape Gardening

Equally useful will the air photograph become to the landscape gardener and architect. Heretofore, in order to get a comprehensive conception of his task and a definite picture of its completion, the landscape gardener has had to depend upon the use of maps and such views as could be made by the sketch artist or the ordinary lateral photograph. In the future, from vertical and oblique photographs of the area to be developed, he will have the means of studying its features in their correct proportions and relationship. By means of similar photographs of completed projects he can choose and combine until he has developed the plans best suited to his purpose. He can bring to his

FIG. 5 Monument Avenue, Richmond, Va., and the statue of Robert E. Lee. An oblique photograph illustrating the use of aerial photography in landscape gardening and street planning.

aid first-hand studies of gardens and grounds the world over whose beauties have made them famous.

ENGINEERING PROJECTS COVERING LARGE AREAS

Where the project covers large areas, the "mosaic," or group of matched photographs, can be used in the study of problems of construction or improvement. Figure 13, a mosaic of the Anacostia flats, the site of improvements under way in the District of Columbia, shows the Anacostia marshes as they appeared in the autumn of 1920, after the changes effected since 1915, as can be seen by comparison with Figure 14, the topographic map of the same area. To the right is the terraced slope rising to a height of about 150 feet above the river—an elevation

FIG. 6—The United States Naval Observatory and grounds, Washington, D. C., as seen from an airplane at a height of a few hundred feet above the ground, showing an unusually attractive arrangement of shrubbery and trees.

so low that the air photograph does not properly reproduce it. Near the foot of the principal terrace lie the tracks of the Pennsylvania Railroad, on which can be seen Benning, Deanewood, and Kenilworth. Between the railroad and the Anacostia River are the Benning race track and the swampy lowland and tidal marshes of the Anacostia flats. The river and the marshland on either side of it from the Pennsylvania Avenue Bridge to Benning Road have been modified by dredging, but north of

Fig. 8—The New York Connecting Railroad Bridge, which affords an all-rail passenger and freight route between Boston and Washington. The bridge, which was completed in 1917, starts on the mainland in the Port Morris section of southern Bronx Borough, New York City, seen in the background, then crosses Bronx Kill, Randalls Island, Little Hell Gate, Wards Island, and Hell Gate to reach the Long Island shore, seen in the extreme lower right corner, at Long Island City, Queens Borough. The tracks continue towards Washington by way of tunnels under the East River and the Hudson.

FIG. 9—A part of Washington, D. C., showing the White House, Treasury, State-War-Navy, and other public buildings in the foreground; the Ellipse, Washington Monument, and new War and Navy offices in the middle ground; and the Tidal Basin, Potomac Park, and the Potomac River in the distance. By no other means could so informative a glimpse be given of a spot of such wide interest. Every feature in the picture is more or less familiar to a large number of Americans, but their familiarity is with the individual features rather than with their situation and relation to one another as shown here.

FIG. 11—Landscape gardening. An airplane view of a part of Long Branch, N. J., taken from a height of 10,000 feet, showing the beach and surf at the right, and the streets, mansions, driveways, and lawns in the body of the picture—an example of the development of a barrier beach of little value before the exploitation for summer homes. Scale, about 1 : 15,000.

this road the surface appears in its natural state. In the mosaic are shown at the left the highlands west of the marshes, wooded in some places but cleared and improved in others. In the northern part can be seen land wooded north of the District line but cleared south of it. So comprehensive a view of the field of the project and of the progress to date should be of great service to the engineers and promoters.

CHAPTER IV

THE MOSAIC

(FIGS. 13 AND 22)

In its simplest form, the mosaic is made by mounting overlapping prints so that the corresponding details coincide. This type of mosaic is quite adequate for relatively small areas or where a high degree of accuracy is not required. For larger areas and greater accuracy, an accurate outline map is used as a base upon which the prints are mounted so that recognizable features coincide with their location on the map. When the prints are properly arranged, the better print of each overlapping pair is selected, the excess paper removed, and the whole mounted and photographed. Figure 13 is left untrimmed to illustrate the method of matching the overlapping prints. The differences in shade are due to difference in printing and developing the pictures which make up the mosaic. The slight offsetting of line at the junction of the prints may be due to errors in mounting, shrinking, or stretching of the photographic paper, tilting of the camera at the time of exposure, or other cause. Such errors and imperfections illustrate the difficulty of using these photographs in the making of maps.

A skillful manipulation of both airplane and camera is necessary to the success of the mosaic. To prevent distortion and variation of scale, the camera must be maintained at the same altitude at all times and pointed directly downward. This can be accomplished by flying with an even keel at a uniform altitude. Mechanical devices are also being perfected to accomplish the same result. Still greater skill is necessary when consecutive rows of exposures are made for the purpose of placing strips of photographs side by side to cover a large area. It is difficult under the varying conditions of wind and weather to fly so evenly and so nearly at the same level that distortions and differences in scale are not noticeable. Strong objection to the mosaic is frequently raised because of inaccuracies due to difference in scale in neighboring prints. Until these defects are overcome, such a group of matched photographs cannot take the place of an accurate map. Much, however, is being done to correct these defects, and, even in photographs where inaccuracies in scale are many, the value of the photograph for the portrayal of detail cannot be denied.

CHAPTER V

GENERAL ASPECTS OF THE SURFACE AS SEEN FROM THE AIR

(FIGS. 12 TO 18)

When a region is viewed from an altitude of several thousand feet the observer can readily imagine himself looking down on a large map. The chief features stand out prominently, the smaller to a lesser degree. Mountains, rivers, and the seashore are espe-

FIG. 12 Benning, D. C., and the Anacostia River, showing, from right to left, cultivated lands 40 to 20 feet above sea level, an elevation too slight to be shown in a vertical photograph; a brushy slope running from 20 feet to sea level; and marsh land along the stream. The checkered pattern of the upland fields is caused by different-colored crops. Shocks of corn, spaced evenly in rows, buildings and shade trees, and light-colored roads and a race track are shown. The light-colored areas along the stream are occupied by tidal marsh and are free from brush but covered with vegetation of annual growth. The figure is one of the photographs used to make the mosaic shown on Fig. 13. It should be compared with Fig. 13 and with the topographic map, Fig. 14. Scale, 1: 11,000.

Fig. 13

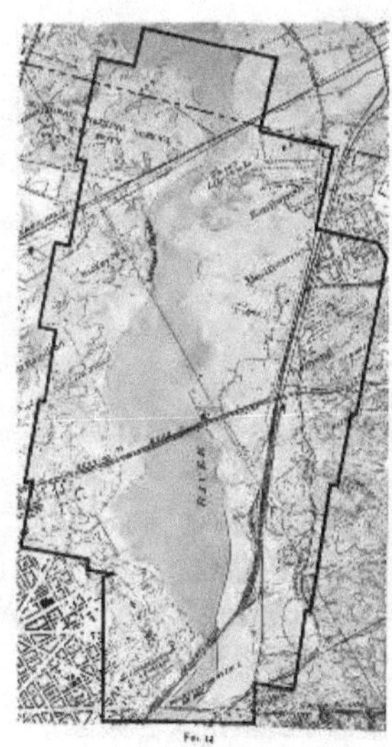

Fig. 14

Fig. 13.—Vertical photograph of the land along the Anacostia River on the eastern edge of Washington, D. C., made up of several photographs matched together and adjusted to points located by ordinary survey methods, and reduced in size to correspond with the map, Fig. 14. The photographs were taken from an airplane with a vertical mapping camera at such intervals of time that the prints overlap, thus making it possible to adjust them to each other and to form a continuous picture of the area. The region shown is the site of improvements that are at present under way, namely the reclamation of the Anacostia River. The channel has been widened by dredging and part of the bordering marsh areas filled in. The photograph shows that this work had progressed to the Benning Road bridge by the autumn of [illegible], when the photograph was taken, while in [illegible], when the area was surveyed for the map, it had been carried out only as far as the Pennsylvania Avenue bridge. Such airplane photographs furnish an incomparable tool in the handling of large-scale engineering projects, both in the study of the territory in its unimproved state and to follow the progress of the work after operations are under way. Scale, about 1:36,000.

Fig. 14. Part of the topographic map of Washington and Vicinity, 1:[illegible], published by the U. S. Geological Survey, showing within the heavy dashed line the same area shown in Fig. 13. Scale, 1:36,000.

cially conspicuous. Streams appear as smooth, winding ribbons—glistening if the sunlight reflected from them enters the eye, dark if the bright rays are reflected away from the eye. Railroads can easily be traced and towns recognized by their form. Concrete roads and others of light-colored material are plainly visible. Those built of dark-colored material appear less prominently. Something even of the character of the forests can be ascertained— whether evenly timbered or partly of primary and partly of secondary growth; whether intact or partly burned over; whether consisting chiefly of one species of trees or of many. The cultivated fields and their relations to roads, streams, and forests are conspicuous. Towns and cities are spread out like panoramic views in which are strikingly visible the residence and manufacturing centers, the layout of streets, the systems of parks, the position of suburbs, and the relation of these to routes of transportation and travel—roads, railroads, and waterways. These and many other features of the landscape—swamps, marshes, buildings, trees, orchards, and many lesser details—are recognizable and are all recorded on the

FIG. 15 (on page 24)—Mosaic of the southeastern part of Mulberry Island, on the left bank of the James River about 11 miles northwest of Newport News, Va., showing an area portrayed by many photographs matched together. Slight differences in shade indicate the junction of the separate prints. The higher land, about 10 feet above sea level as determined by surveys on the ground, is shown at the right by roads and cultivated fields. It is to be noted that roads outline the dividing line between the high ground and the marsh. At the left are lower areas of wooded or brushy swampland and of grassy marsh. They contain a number of abandoned channels: some completely silted up, others containing small thoroughfares, and still others drained by meandering streams which seem to have developed after the channels were definitely abandoned by the streams which originally occupied them.

The streams which drain the marshes have many characteristics of streams which drain higher lands. They have dendritic patterns, so called from resemblance to the forking branches of a tree; channels which widen downstream; and winding or meandering courses. The island terminates in a long spit composed of silt and fine sand. The banks to the left on James River are low and marshy; those to the right on Warwick Creek, except for one small marsh, form low bluffs.

In order that the mosaic may be compared with the map, Fig. 16, it has been placed with the northerly part at the top of the page, with the result that, until the page is reversed, the trees in the swampland appear like hollows in the earth. Scale, 1: 14,000.

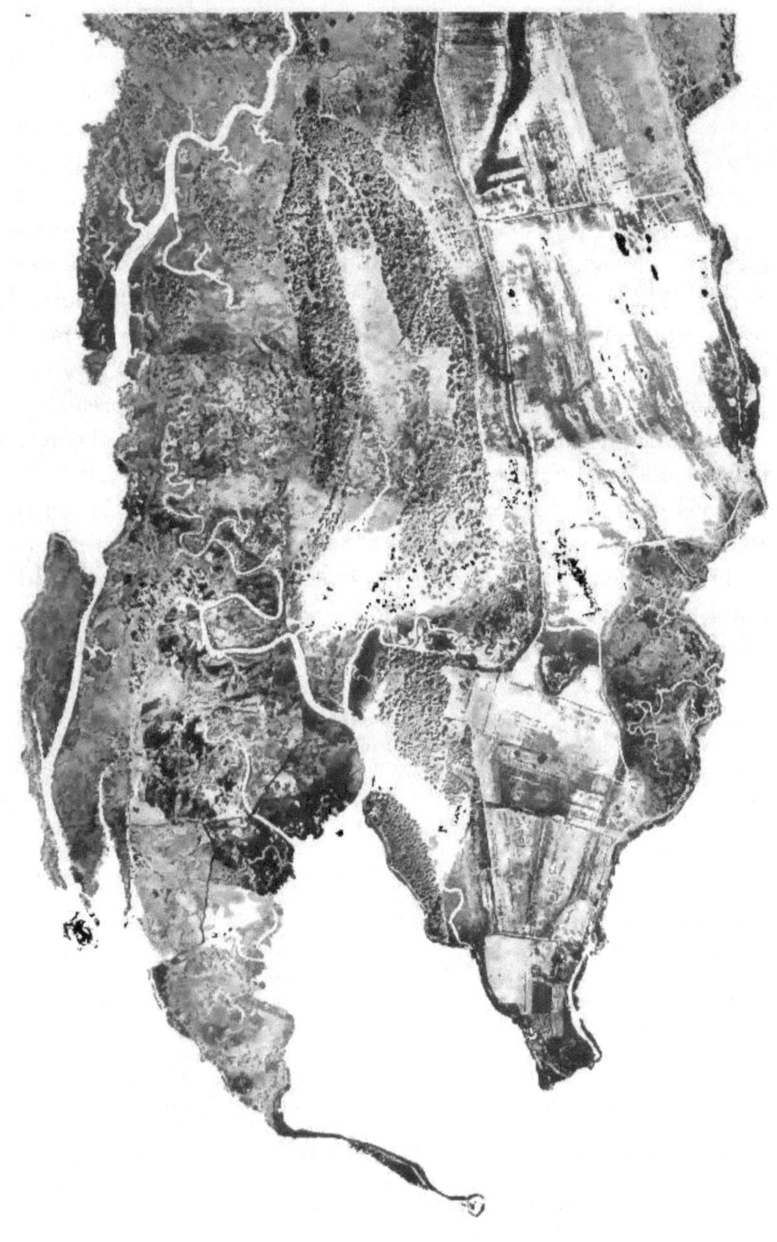

FIG. 16—The same area as shown in Fig. 15 reduced from a section of a map on the scale of 1:10,000 by the Corps of Engineers, U. S. A. The photographs shown in Fig. 15 were used for mapping certain small features on this map, such as small streams. Scale, 1: 14,000.

photographic negative. So faithfully does the camera reproduce all the horizontal features within its range of vision that it is conceivable that a photograph correctly dated might become a valuable record in cases of boundary disputes or other litigations involving the position of fences, fields, roads, or even streams, at a given date.

Fig. 17

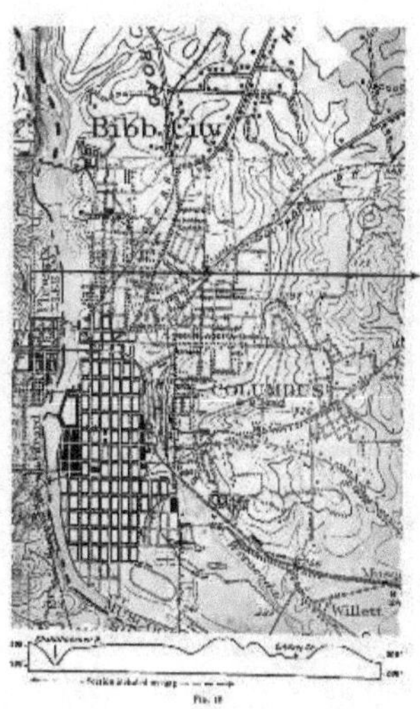

Fig. 18

Fig. 17. Columbus, Ga. [illegible]

Fig. 18.—Map of the same area shown in Fig. 17 [illegible]

CHAPTER VI

MARSHES AND MARSH DRAINAGE

(FIGS. 19 TO 27)

Mention has been made of the objects seen better from the air than from any viewpoint on the ground; but there are some objects which as a whole can be seen only from above. Swamps, parts of everglades, peaks in the midst of difficult country, precipitous canyon walls, and many volcanic craters cannot be seen from the ground without undue effort. Photographs of bluffs, terraces, and other slopes facing bodies of water have hitherto been adequately obtainable only from the water. All of these can be readily viewed and photographed from the airplane. Pictorial representations of drainage systems were rare until photographs such as Figure 19 were taken from airplanes. The intricate drainage of marshes like those along the Pamunkey River in Virginia pictured in Figure 20 was never accurately shown until photographed from the air.

Of frequent occurrence on the Atlantic Coastal Plain of the United States are swamps and marshes inaccessible from the ground. Much of the surface material is so soft that they cannot be easily traversed; and, even where firm enough to support a man's weight, few of the details are deemed of sufficient importance to warrant the trouble and expense of mapping by ordinary methods. Yet the trapper would scarcely admit that these details are unimportant, and, to the student, they are an interesting feature of marsh topography that has thus far received little attention.

Figure 25 is part of the excellent New Kent, Va., sheet of the topographic map and is probably as detailed as a map of this character should be when made from ground surveys only. However, on comparison of the map with a photo-

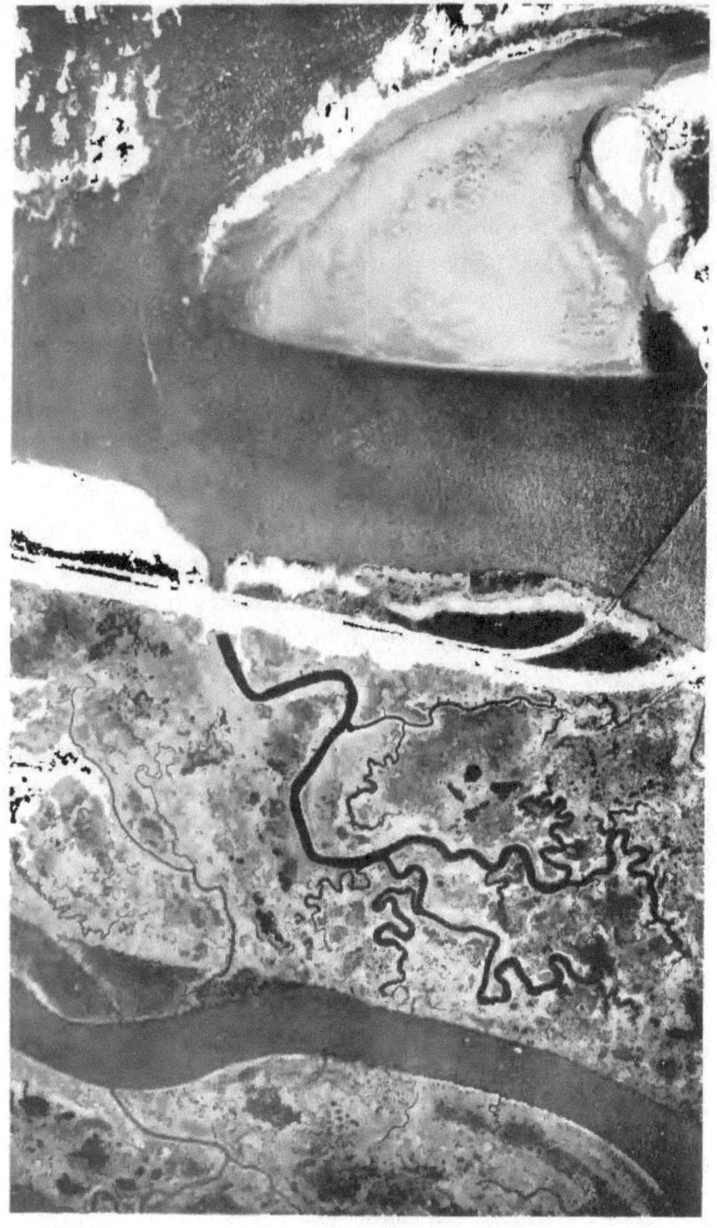

graph of the same area (Fig. 24), there is no difficulty in detecting errors; and it is probable that, had the photograph been available when the map was made, the marshes would have been represented differently.

Marsh Drainage

One of the most striking characteristics of marsh topography illustrated by the photographs presented here is the great wealth of drainage lines and the resemblance of the drainage patterns to those of river systems developed on higher ground. The dendritic patterns, the meanders, and the sharply outlined divides are surprising in areas which have altitudes varying from only a few inches to a little more than a foot at times of ordinary high tide and which are wholly submerged at times of maximum tide. Some of the streams have gently winding courses suggestive of normal stream development. Others, particularly the smaller, have a conspicuous angularity of course. It is possible that the latter may have originated as the trails of animals. Some of the lines are observed to cross the larger streams and are probably tracks made by muskrats. Some of the streams rise close to the river's brink and lead to through-going waterways near the center of the marsh. This suggests the deposition of silt on the brink of the river at times of high water. The notched appearance of the shore in Figure 20 seems to be due to overhanging bunches of sedge grass and, in some instances, to the breaking away of the surface mat or crust of the marsh formed by the interlacing roots of grass. The mottled appearance of the marsh in this picture may be partly due to shadow of clouds, but to some extent, at least, the difference in shade is caused by differences in the character of the plants.

The marshes used for illustration here are typical of many along the Atlantic Coast. They are situated near West Point, Va. The Pamunkey and the Mattaponi Rivers both rise in the Piedmont Plateau, flow southeastward through the tidewater

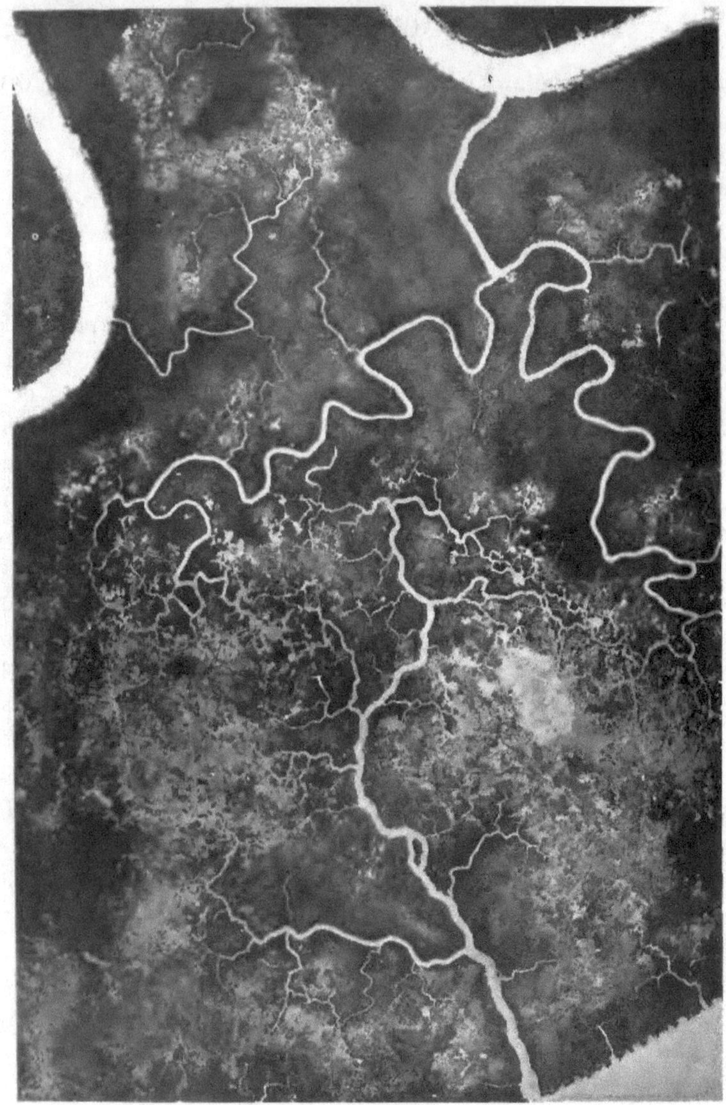

FIG. 20 Details of marshland. A part of Lee Marsh near West Point, Va. (cf. Fig. 26), as photographed from a height of 2,000 feet, June, 1920. Local observers report that this marsh has been submerged only twice in nineteen years. The drainage systems are well entrenched. The larger stream channels are cut 1 to 5 feet or more below low tide (the tidal variation at West Point is about 3.4 feet), and their form is made stable by the tough surface crust of the marsh, consisting of the matted roots of the luxuriant sedge grass. The intricate, veinlike appearance of the drainage lines and the furry appearance of the edges of all the waterways, showing overhanging vegetation, are of interest. Drainage systems flowing in opposite directions show connecting tributaries apparently silted up. Scale, about 1 : 4,000.

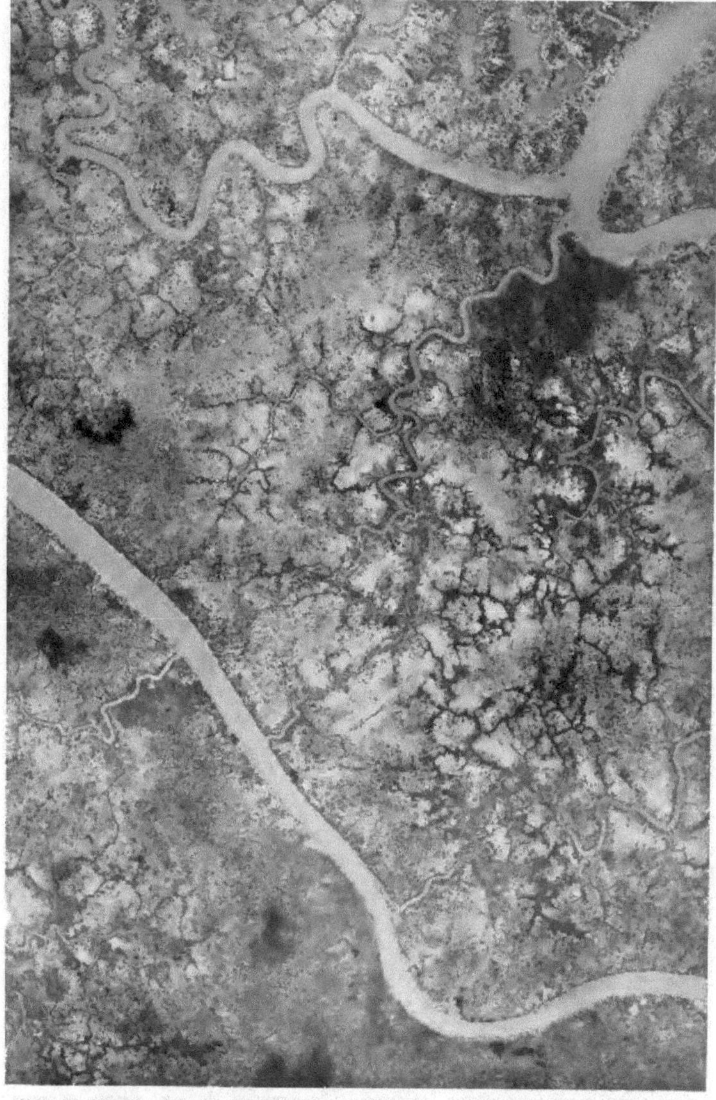

FIG. 21—Details of frequently submerged marshland. A part of Cousaic Marsh on the Pamunkey River, near Sweet Hall, Va. (cf. Fig. 24), as photographed from a height of 2,000 feet, June, 1920. The surface of the marsh is covered with water several times each year, according to local report. It is relatively soft, and a comparison with Fig. 20 shows an apparently different, less dense vegetation than that of Lee Marsh, which is rarely submerged. The stream channels are less definitely fixed and lack the evidence of overhanging vegetation. Scale, about 1:4,000.

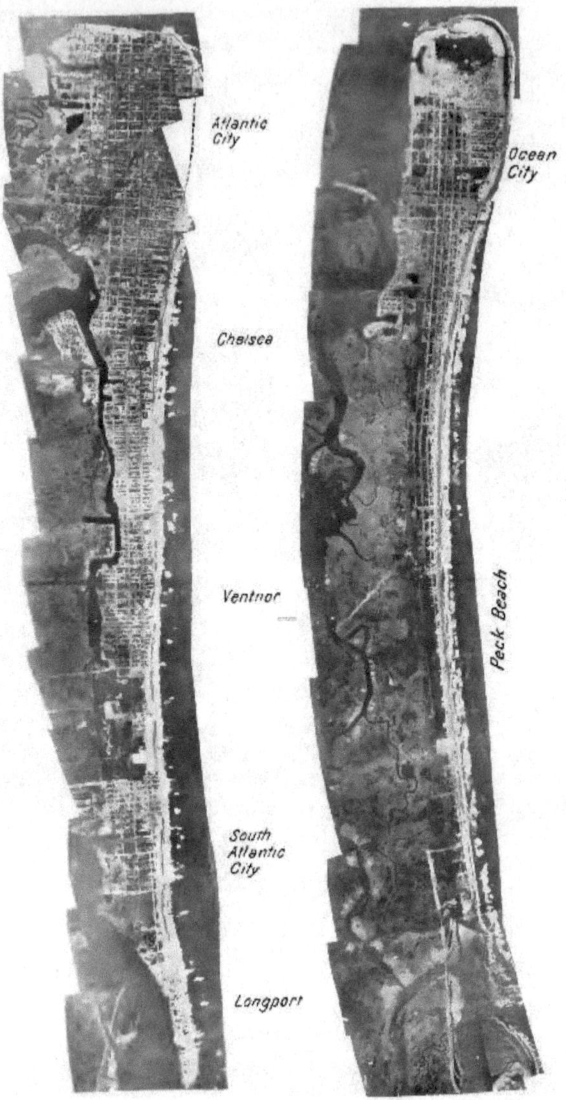

FIG. 22.—Atlantic City and Ocean City, N. J. Strips of photographs taken from an airplane, March, 1920, from a height of 10,000 feet, showing, in order from east to west: the ocean water, which appears dark-colored; the surf, white where it breaks into foam; the light-colored beach sand; the cities laid out on the sand of the barrier beach; and the marshes, channels, and drainage systems west of the barrier. West of Peck Beach in the strip of photograph at the right many features characteristic of salt marsh areas of the Coastal Plain are shown back of the barrier beach. The right strip forms the southern continuation of the left strip. Scale, about 1:75,000.

FIG. 23 A river system in miniature. A small stream near Hampton, Va., showing flood plain, meanders, an ox-bow lake and cut-off, abandoned channels and a delta partly under water. Scale, not known.

FIG. 24—Sweet Hall Marsh on the lower Pamunkey River, near West Point, Va., as photographed from a height of 10,000 feet at 11 A. M., December 11, 1920. Cousaic Marsh lies to the left and Hill Marsh to the right of the central meander. Some of the water-courses in these marshes are thoroughfares, or channels opening to the river at both ends, that can be traversed by boat at high tide. But many of them are quite different in nature, beginning as minute rills and broadening toward the mouth in a manner suggesting typical drainage channels on higher land. Scale, about 1:31,000.

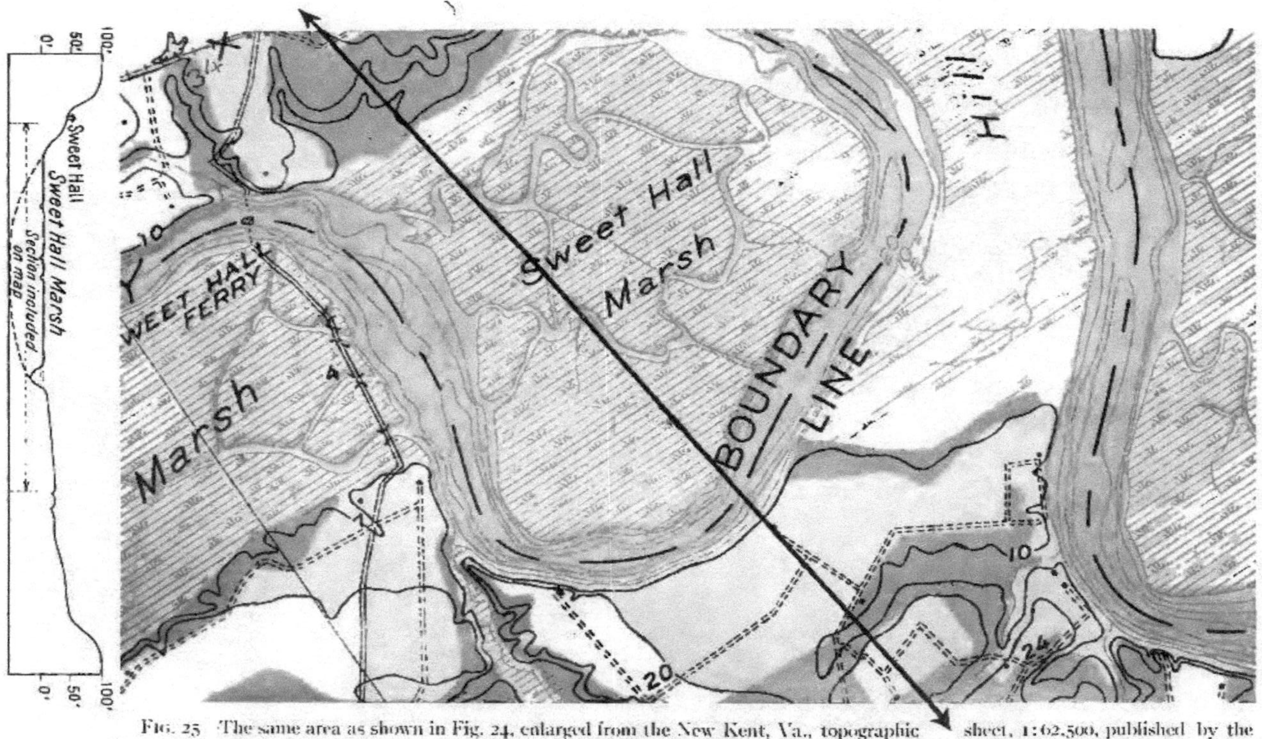

FIG. 25 The same area as shown in Fig. 24, enlarged from the New Kent, Va., topographic sheet, 1:62,500, published by the U. S. Geological Survey. The cross section at the left lies along the line indicated on the map and extends somewhat beyond its borders. The somewhat greater height of the map than of the photograph, although both cover exactly the same area, is due to the unavoidable slight difference in tilt of each of the exposures of which the photographic mosaic is made up. This illustrates the fact that airplane photographs cannot be directly used as equivalent to maps, until the necessary adjustments have been made. Experiments in camera construction are under way to overcome these difficulties by automatic devices. Scale, 1:31,000.

FIG. 26 Eltham Marsh on the lower Pamunkey River, as photographed from an altitude of about 10,000 feet at 11 A. M., December 11, 1920. At the right lies the town of West Point, Va., at the junction of the Mattaponi and Pamunkey Rivers, and at the left appears a part of Lee Marsh. Eltham Marsh, in the center of the illustration, is traversed by a so-called thoroughfare, through which boats of light draft make their way at high tide. At one point in the middle of the marsh the thoroughfare is perceptibly broader than elsewhere, and the tidal currents entering from opposite ends of the thoroughfare meet there and cause slack water in which silt is deposited, forming mud flats exposed at low tide. The cultivated fields south of the marsh are on a bench about 10 feet higher than the marsh. Scale, about 1:31,000.

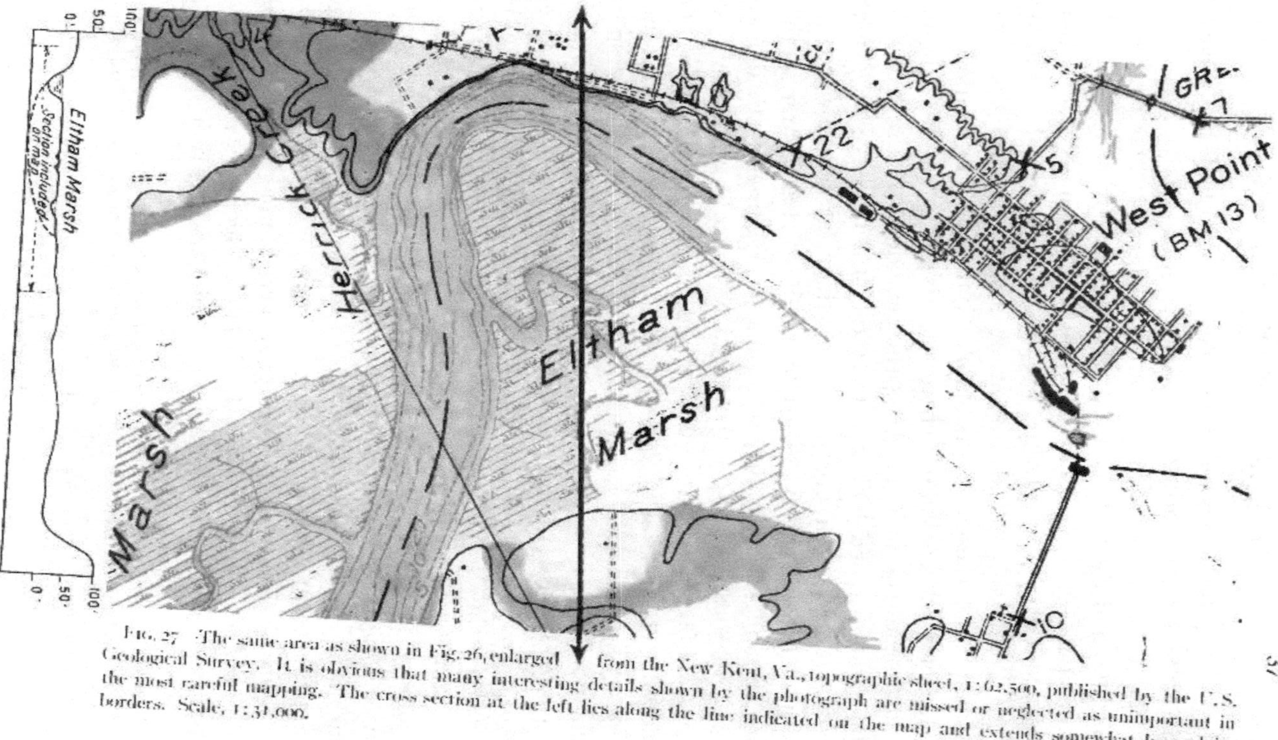

FIG. 27 The same area as shown in Fig. 26, enlarged from the New Kent, Va., topographic sheet, 1:62,500, published by the U.S. Geological Survey. It is obvious that many interesting details shown by the photograph are missed or neglected as unimportant in the most careful mapping. The cross section at the left lies along the line indicated on the map and extends somewhat beyond its borders. Scale, 1:31,000.

portion of Virginia, and join about midway of the Coastal Plain to form the York River[1] (see Fig. 58).

The York is one of the estuaries of the tidewater portion of Virginia, and the water level at West Point, the junction of the two tributaries, rises and falls about 3½ feet under tidal action. The Pamunkey is affected by the tide 53 miles by channel above West Point, and the Mattaponi 42 miles. Much of the broad lowland along these rivers is marshy, but the largest marshes are found near West Point, where the river current in swinging from side to side has formed great meanders. For some reason the valleys eroded long ago by these streams have filled with sediment here to a greater extent than farther downstream; perhaps because this is essentially the head of sea water, so that the checking of the current of the river causes it to deposit much of its load. Sea water regularly mingles with the river water as far upstream as West Point, but above this point the water is chiefly fresh. The marshes consist of soft mud and muck to a considerable depth. A well driven in Hill Marsh to an underlying artesian horizon penetrated 50 feet of this soft material before entering rock such as is exposed in the river bank. The thickness of the mud is comparable to the maximum depth of the York farther downstream and suggests that the old valley which there is filled with water is here filled to a depth of 50 feet or more with sediment brought down by the river. Only a small part of the marsh near the landward margin has surface material firm enough to support the weight of large animals except when the surface is frozen.

Many kinds of marsh plants grow here, among which is sedge grass (*Spartina cynosuroides* (L.) Willd.), which grows to a height of 10 feet or more and forms dense thickets. Its roots interlace

[1] The Pamunkey gets its name from a tribe of Indians famous in the early days of Virginian history but now reduced to a few families living on a reservation situated on the banks of the river near Lester Manor. Mattaponi is a combination name. The Mat and the Ta unite to form Matta Creek. The Matta and the Po unite, and Ny Creek is a tributary to the Po. The waters of these streams unite to form the river, and the names Mat, Ta, Po, and Ny unite to form its name—Mattaponi.

to form a tough mat which in some places will support the weight of a man. In other places the soft muck reaches to the surface.

"Thoroughfares"

These marshes are cut by a few waterways open at both ends known as thoroughfares, or tidal runs, which also serve as the trunk streams through which the marsh is drained. Some of the thoroughfares may be trunk streams modified by tides, or they may be silted remnants of abandoned river channels. Some seem to be channels in the last stages of silting. The incoming tide enters the down-river end but ascends the thoroughfare more slowly than it ascends the river. The tide in the river reaches the upper end of the thoroughfare, enters it, and meets the opposing tide within the marsh near the upstream end of the passageway. Where the tides meet, thus causing slack water, silt is deposited and mud flats are formed. In Eltham Marsh (Fig. 26) these flats are well within the marsh. In the larger thoroughfares of Sweet Hall Marsh (Fig. 24) the tide passes entirely through while the tide in the river is making its long way around, so that slack water and the deposition of silt occur at the extreme upper end of the passage. In all of the thoroughfares the silting has reached the stage that precludes their use by boat, except at times of high water. Even at high tide some are navigable only by small skiffs, although throughout much of the course the water is many feet deep.

Some of the thoroughfares become narrow and shallow upstream in a manner that suggests that they originate as two normal streams flowing in opposite directions from a common point and that they were later united by the breaking down of the divide between their headwaters. Such a junction might be affected by an unusually high tide breaking through a divide and cutting a channel. Such a divide, be it noted, consists of soft mud only a few inches above the general level and might readily be broken down. In some instances the connection may have originated as an animal trail, as we have seen. Muskrats, otters, and other marsh animals use the waterways as lines of travel and make paths in between them from one to another. Apparently many of the small drainage lines originated in this way, but in some instances stream systems of considerable size and complexity are independent of all others and possess all the characteristics of normally developed river systems.

CHAPTER VII

COASTAL MUD FLATS

(FIGS. 28 AND 29)

Of frequent occurrence along the Atlantic Coast of the United States are low mud flats which are practically at sea level and which are covered with water at times of high tide. Where these tracts are exposed to the air during ebb tide for so short a time that plants have not taken root and where the surface material is fine-grained and soft, the tracts are known as mud flats. In the part of the peninsula between Delaware and Chesapeake Bays belonging to the state of Virginia which is called the Eastern Shore a low barrier beach of sand has formed on the ocean side several miles off shore, and the space between this and the mainland is occupied by mud flats, broad, shallow lagoons, and an intricate maze of interlacing channels and winding, branching, interlocking, vermicular streams.

The mud flats are exposed for a short time during low tide, and, as the surface of the water here rises and falls with the tide more than 4 feet, with a maximum fluctuation considerably greater, large volumes of water are continually flowing backward and forward over the flats. As the tide rises, strong currents of sea water set in through the inlets, flow up the main channels and through the thoroughfares, and gradually find their way into the countless small channels and out of them over the broad level stretches of soft mud. As the tide falls, this action is reversed, and the broad sheet of water finds its way by devious paths through the winding watercourses out to sea. The larger channels extend considerably below the surface at times of highest water and may be quite deep even at times of low water. They are, perhaps, stream courses excavated before the region was drowned. Many of the smaller channels also have the general form characteristic of normal stream channels, although others show peculiarities not common to subaerial drainage. The origin of these submarine and tidal features is not well understood, but the photographs of them show their form and furnish some basis for a study of them.

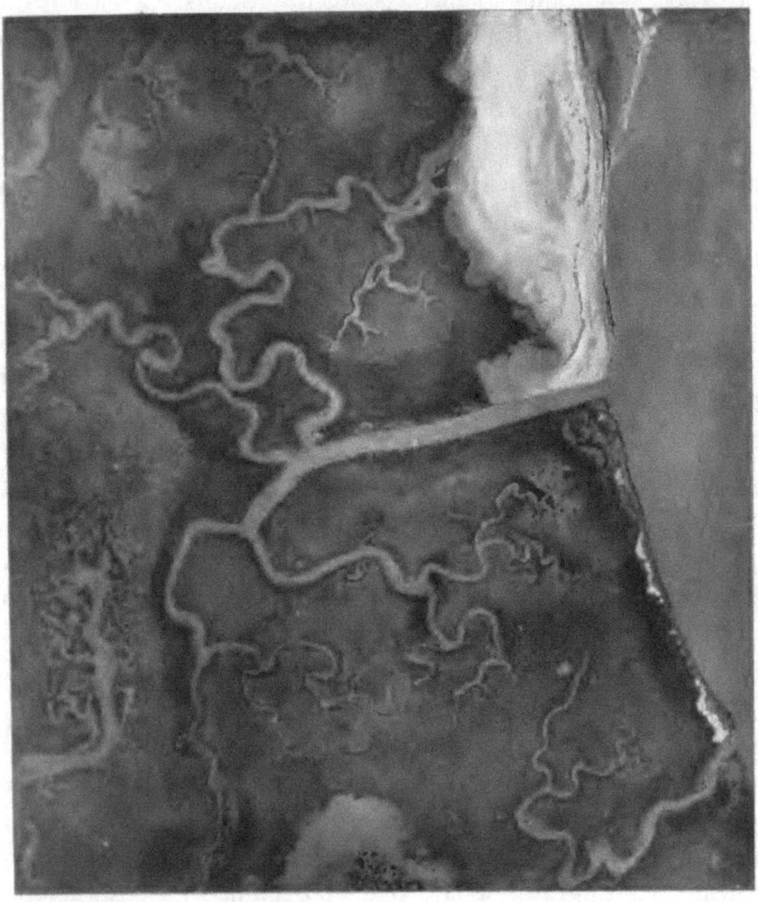

FIG. 28—A stream system of the mud-flat area on the ocean side of the Eastern Shore, Virginia. The light-colored area is beach sand above water. The treelike form is a stream system of subnormally developed pattern. Note the seeming uncertainty of course, some of the branch streams rising close to the mouth of the trunk stream; the junction of branches at the head; and the "frostwork" patterns. Scale not known.

The photographs reproduced as Figures 28 and 29 were taken northeast of Cape Charles, Virginia, in the summer of 1920 at low tide. The light-colored ribbon-like bands represent water-filled channels; and the darker-colored areas, either wet mud ex-

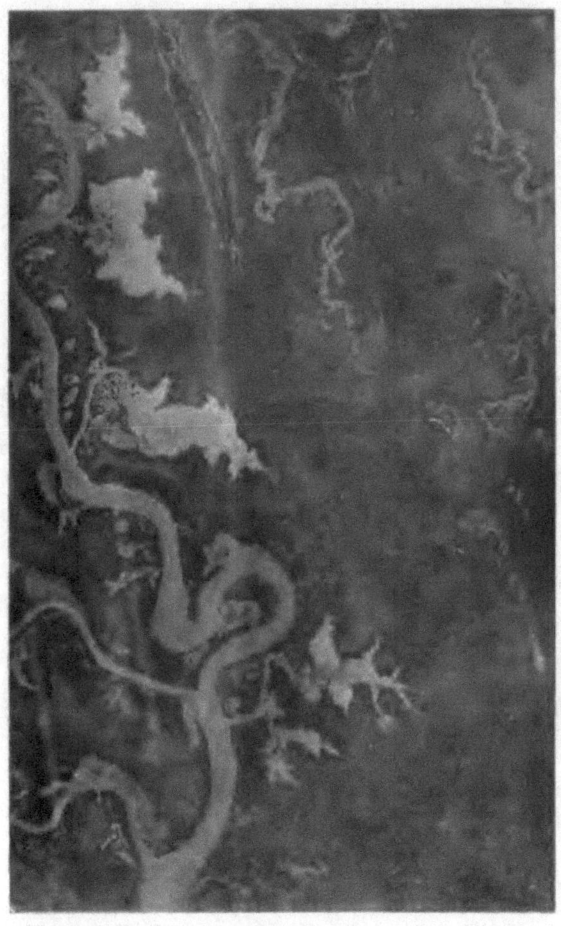

FIG. 29—Mud-flat streams, showing curious frostwork pattern at the head of underwater channels. Note the pools and the veinlike drainage lines from them. Scale not known.

posed to the air or mud slightly submerged. However, photographs taken under certain conditions of light may show the exact line between the exposed and the drowned portions of a land surface.

CHAPTER VIII

SUBMERGED LAND FORMS

(FIGS. 30 TO 33)

Heretofore the study of beaches, deltas, and other partly submerged land forms has been chiefly confined to the exposed parts, the underwater forms being largely matters of conjecture. By means of air photographs not only can the exposed parts of the delta and beach be studied, but the forms of shoals and terraces, the underwater portions of river deltas, tidal deltas and their underwater distributaries, and many other submerged forms can be shown clearly. Sand bars, terraces, and other submerged forms appear in many of the photographs already presented; but a few so taken that the bars and terraces appear to be the chief objects in the picture may be useful for illustrating the underwater land forms and for demonstrating that these forms can be successfully photographed. Unfortunately not many photographs could be found which were taken with the express object in view of illustrating underwater land features. In most of the available photographs these features were only incidental, the chief purpose in taking them being to photograph the shore.

Much has been written concerning the physiographic history of the Atlantic Coastal Plain of the United States, and the question is still being debated whether the land is rising, sinking, or stationary. To some extent these questions are answered by the exposed land forms. The submarine forms are imperfectly known. The possibility of recognizing shoals and channels from a photograph and of determining in some measure the shapes of the submerged land forms opens a new avenue of approach to the study of submarine geography. In some places, especially in regions of drowned topography, it is possible that, by using the air photograph in working out the physiographic processes that have produced the land forms that are now under water, some of the vexing problems of earth history may be solved.

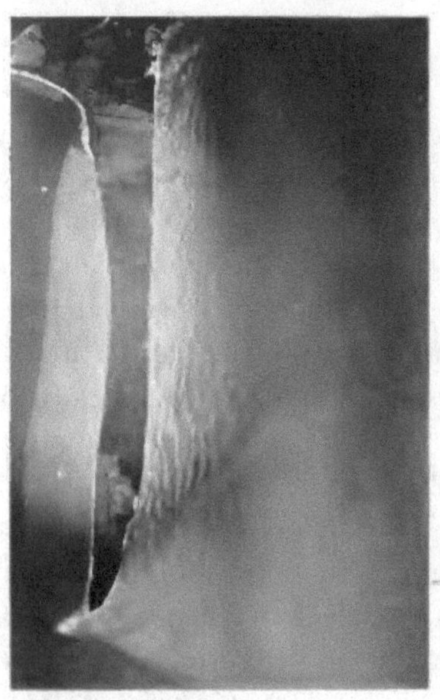

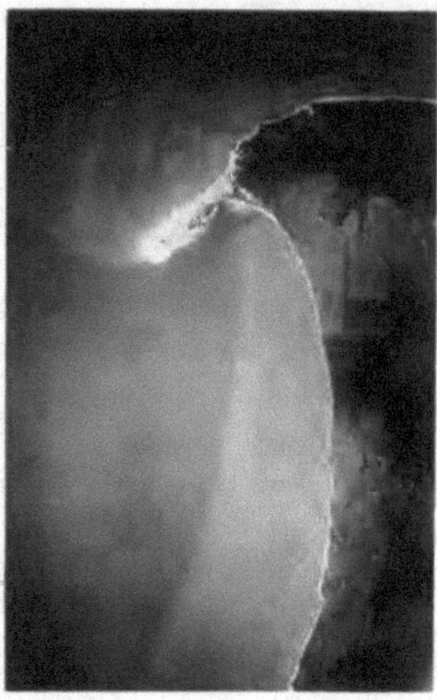

Fig. 30 (left)- Sand bars and drowned terrace about Stove Point Neck, at the mouth of the Piankatank River, Virginia, as photographed from a height of about 10,000 feet at 11:30 A. M., December 11, 1920. West (left) of the neck, at the outer edge of the terrace, the water is 2 to 3 feet deep at low tide, or 5.7 feet and 6.7 feet at high tide, but deepens abruptly westward, where it is 20 to 30 feet deep in Fishing Bay (see Fig. 32). To the south and east of the point the abrupt descent is at the side of the deep channel of the Piankatank River. To the right, the bottom, having a wavy appearance because of sand bars, fades off more gradually under deep water. The mottled area in the middle of the neck is wooded, and the smoother parts near the point and in the upper part of the neck are cleared land. Scale, about 1:30,000.

Fig. 31 (right)—Drowned terraces at Gwynn Island at the mouth of the Piankatank River, Virginia, as photographed from a height of about 10,000 feet at 11:30 A. M., December 11, 1920. At the right is a part of the island, showing trees, fields, and houses. Bordering the land area is a narrow band of light-colored beach sand, expanded at Cherry Point into a conspicuous sharply recurved hook. Under the shallow water can be seen wave marks resembling large ripple marks. The water is 2 to 3 feet deep at low tide at the outer edge of the light-colored submerged shelf, beyond which the bottom descends abruptly toward the left to a depth of about 20 feet. North of Cherry Point the wavy bottom shades off more gradually to the deep channel of the Piankatank. Scale, about 1:30,000.

The Best Conditions for Photographing Underwater Land Forms

The photographic study of underwater land forms is relatively new, and little information concerning it is available. It is annoyingly obvious to the air observer that at times he can see nothing beneath the surface of the water, whereas at other

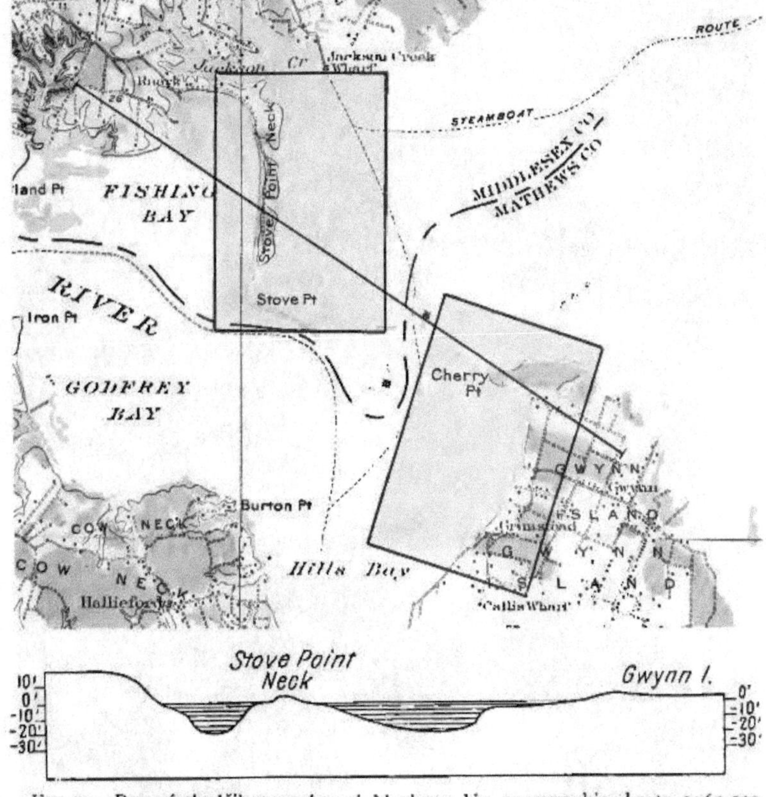

Fig. 32—Part of the Kilmarnock and Mathews, Va., topographic sheets, 1: 62,500. published by the U. S. Geological Survey, showing the location of Figs. 31 and 32; and a cross section along the line indicated on the map, showing a terrace 26 feet above sea level at the left, one less than 5 feet above water level on Gwynn Island, one 5 feet or less below water level; and the river channel with abrupt banks between the shoals. Scale, 1: 70,000.

times he can see with great distinctness. In trying to ascertain the most favorable conditions for such observation, it was found that submerged objects are seen best when the sky is evenly overcast or when it is uniformly clear. Sometimes when the sky is only partly cloudy the surface of the water seems to act as a mirror and nothing is seen but the reflection of cloud and sky. Waves have less effect on the visibility of objects beneath the surface than was expected, although they diffuse the reflected light to some extent and consequently weaken the image on the negative. But the reflected light from the surface of the water is stronger than that coming from objects under water. Hence, to photograph underwater features successfully, a time should be chosen when direct reflection of light from the sun or from a brightly illuminated cloud will not enter the lens.

Experience in both the air and the laboratory shows that the best results are likely to be obtained when the sunlight strikes the surface at an oblique angle. In summer favorable times are mid-forenoon or mid-afternoon under an evenly illuminated sky. In winter the sun is low enough at midday to avoid direct reflection into the lens. But experience also indicates that often photographs taken at moments when the eye caught the image of a submerged object show only the surface of the water.

CHAPTER IX

THE PLAIN FROM THE AIR

(Figs. 34 to 41)

A River on the Great Plains

The difficulty of photographing a plain from a point on its surface needs no emphasis, but its successful representation by means of air photographs is illustrated by many figures in this book. The Great Plains of the west-central part of the United States are illustrated here by a view of the Red River (Fig. 36), which shows the flat surface of the land and the broad sandy bed of the river only partly covered by the intricately woven strands of the braided channels—a scene characteristic of the Great Plains.

Meandering Streams on the Coastal Plain

The ox-bow curves of meandering streams are among the features of the earth's surface most familiar to the student of physical geography; yet, heretofore, they have been illustrated only by maps, constructed at great labor and expense. Comprehensive photographs of them are rare and are, at best, imperfect and unsatisfactory for purposes of illustration. On the other hand, meandering streams lend themselves admirably to air photography. Equally familiar to the student of geography and physiography is the term "abandoned meander." These ancient stream courses, many of which are now occupied by marsh, brush, or forest, have been still more difficult to illustrate by means of photographs. In some instances wooded meanders like those near Columbus, Ga. (Fig. 34), long ago abandoned by the stream that formed them, are shown in air pictures in a manner but little less conspicuous than the meanders of the

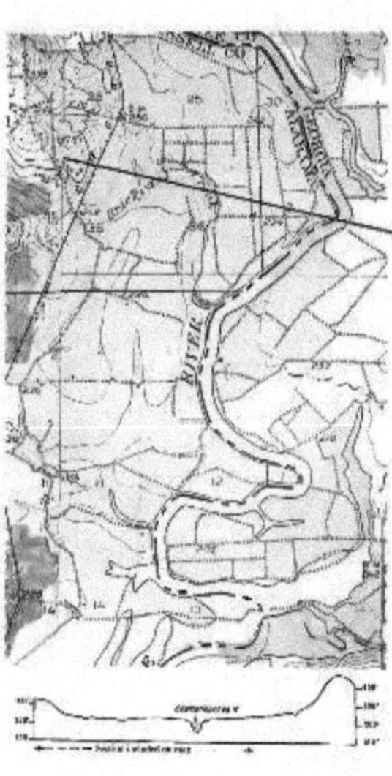

FIG. 37.—A characteristic glacial drift plain in southwestern Michigan. There appear, at the left, the round surface of a terminal moraine and gullied slopes, which show mottled in the picture; morainic hollows and kettleholes once partly filled with water but now filled with peat or occupied by marshes formed by the accumulation of peat from plant growth until carbonaceous matter has replaced the water of the original lake; in the center, a relatively smooth outwash plain characterized by straight roads and well-cultivated fields; and, at the right, a brush-lined creek, a small reservoir, and the town of Flowerfield. Scale, about 1: 20,000.

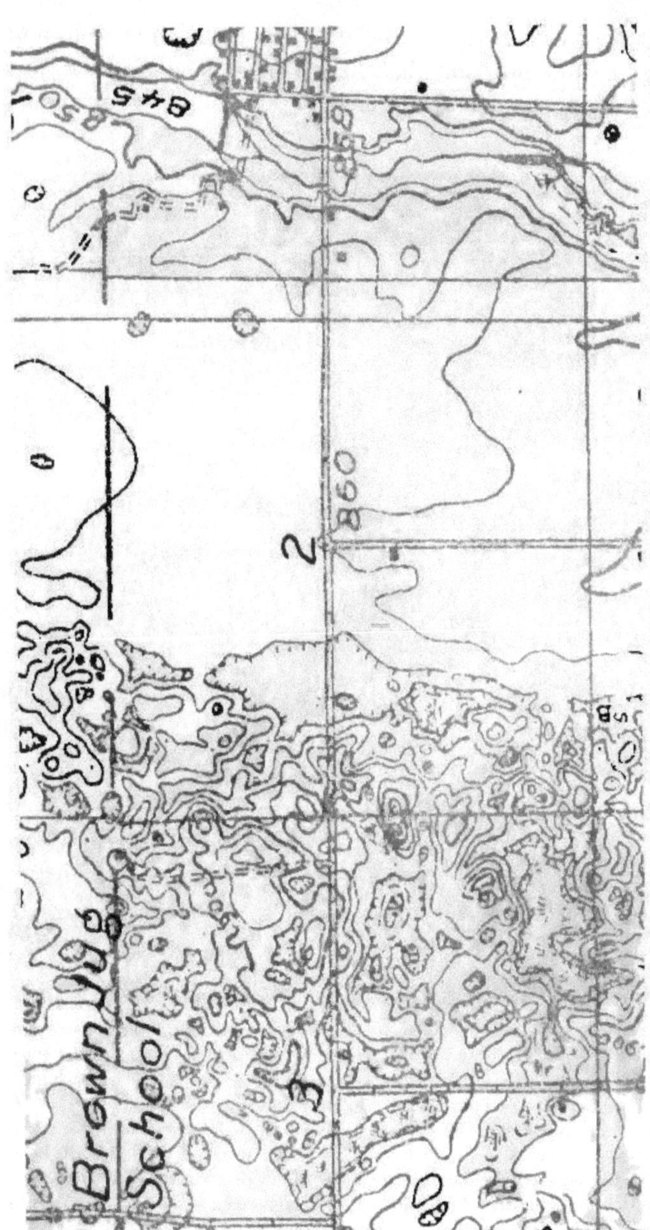

Fig. 38 The same area as shown in Fig. 37, enlarged from the advance edition, 1: 48,000, of the Schoolcraft, Mich., topographic sheet to be published by the U. S. Geological Survey. This advance sheet results from an experiment in the use of airplanes for mapping. The area was photographed with a mapping camera. From the photograph a base map was constructed, which was verified on the ground; on this base the contour lines were added by instrumental survey. Scale, 1: 20,000.

present-day stream. It is believed that instructors will find Figure 34 useful, not only in illustrating meandering streams and abandoned meanders but also in showing how meanders develop.

FIG. 39—Schoolcraft, Mich., a town typical of the agricultural portions of the north-central United States, showing the characteristic features—roads, fields, town blocks, and others—by which the aviator can recognize a locality from a distance. The mottled appearance of the land surrounding the village is characteristic of air photographs of glacial moraine regions. The picture of the village itself might be taken as a prototype of the American village with its fairly regular layout of streets, its business center indicated by a few larger roofs along the widest street, its lawns, trees, and gardens, the bordering farm lands, and the scattered extensions of the village into points in the direction of the main roads. Scale, about 1:14,000.

The Glacial Drift Plain

Some of the characteristics of a third type of plain, the glacial drift plain, are shown in Figures 37 to 41. Here are pictured gla-

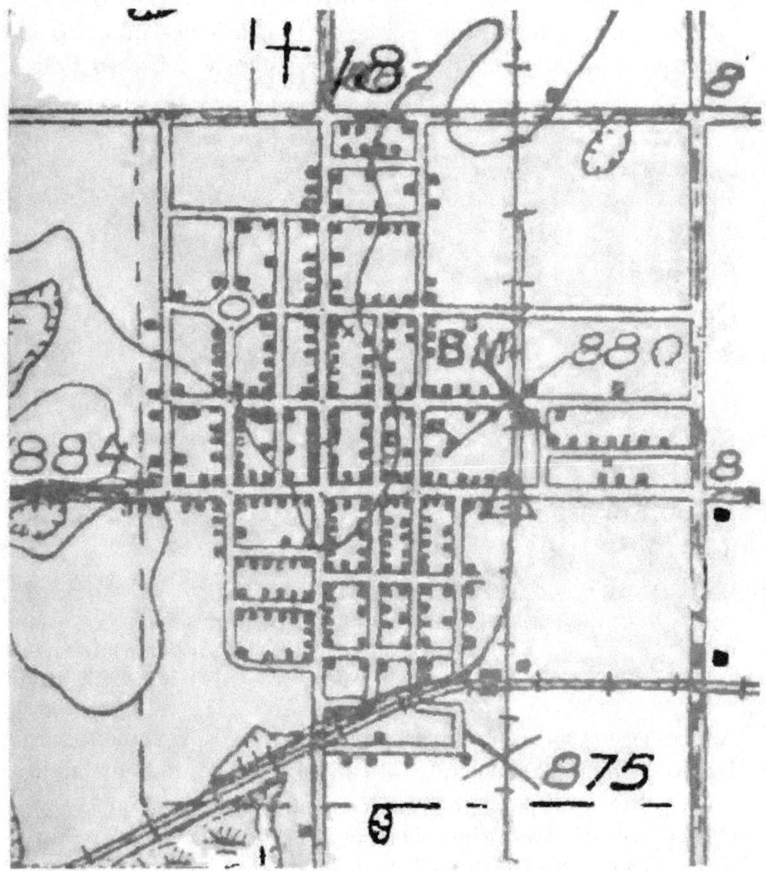

Fig. 40 Map of the town of Schoolcraft, Mich., for comparison with Fig. 39. Enlarged from the advance edition, 1:48,000, of the Schoolcraft, Mich., topographic sheet to be published by the U. S. Geological Survey. Scale, 1:14,000.

cial lakes, bogs, marshes, moraines, and outwash plains, peat-filled depressions, kettleholes and gullied slopes—typical features of a glaciated region. The views show, also, many of the familiar aspects of the central and western parts of the United States: the rectangular pattern formed by the land subdivisions established by the United States Land Office, the checkerboard pattern being emphasized by the section-line roads; the minor subdivisions into fields; and the cultivation of a variety of crops.

These photographs were selected from a series taken as an experiment in map-making. In June, 1920, the United States

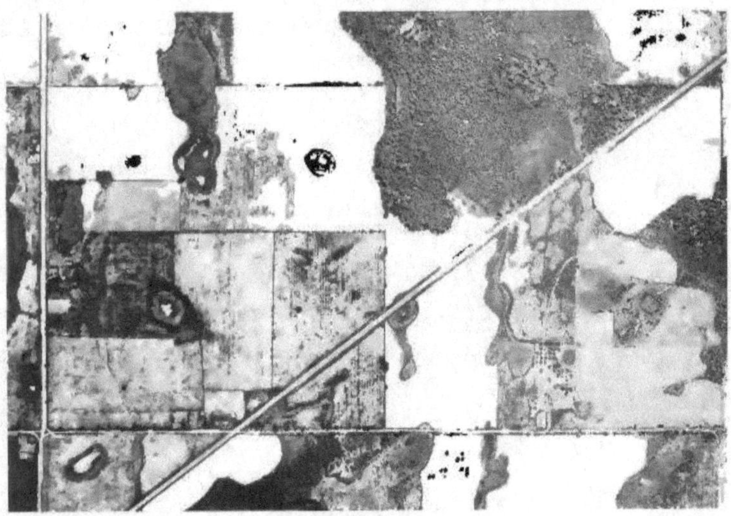

FIG. 41—Kettleholes and other depressions in glacial till, on the Grand Trunk Railway about 5 miles southwest of Schoolcraft, Mich. The distance between the eastern (right) edge of this view and the western (left) of Fig. 37 is about 1 mile. Scale, about 1:15,000.

Air Service sent a plane equipped with a K-1 camera from Dayton, Ohio, to Schoolcraft, Mich., where in seven hours' flying time a fifteen-minute quadrangle, about 220 square miles, was photographed. The prints were matched together and reduced to a scale of 1:48,000. From them such features as roads, streams, forests, land corners, etc., were transferred to plane-table sheets, which the topographic engineers on the ground then used for contouring the relief. Figure 38 is a part of the preliminary proof of this map. It may be added that the experiment is regarded as highly favorable to the use of the airplane camera as an instrument in mapping.

CHAPTER X

MOUNTAIN FEATURES

(Figs. 42 to 52)

In obtaining photographic illustrations from the ground of mountains, canyons, and associated land forms, the same difficulty, but in exaggerated form, is encountered that obtains in securing an advantageous point of view for small objects. The difficulty is overcome in large measure by the use of aircraft. In an airplane the observer can rise above the obstructions which interfere with the view desired; can look an isolated mountain peak squarely in the face, as in the case of the photograph of Mt. Shasta (Fig. 42); can study the details of its ice cap (Fig. 42) and gaze downward on the lateral and recessional moraines left by the retreat of the mountain's glaciers (Fig. 43). Few volcanic craters, occurring as they do at the top of cones, have been successfully photographed unless some higher mountain stands near-by on which a favorable viewpoint can be found. From an airplane, however, one can look into the very throat of a crater, as into that of Cinder Cone (Fig. 48), near Lassen Peak, California.

Much attention has been given to the interrelations of canyons, gorges, and mountain ridges, but these relations have hitherto been illustrated chiefly by means of maps and charts. Figures 49, 50, and 52 picture three relations more expressively than any map. To the experienced geographer a map may illustrate perfectly the action of a stream working headward into higher land; but the student to whom the conception of headward erosion is new will certainly grasp he idea more readily from the picture presented in Figure 52. No map could give so clear a conception of a maturely dissected highland as does a photograph like that of the Santa Monica Mountains (Fig. 50).

Fig. 42—A glaciated volcanic cone: Mt. Shasta, California, 14,162 feet high, as seen by an airplane observer from the northeast, showing Hotlum Glacier in the foreground and Wintun Glacier at the extreme left. The monadnock which separates the two main lobes of Hotlum Glacier appears as the dark-colored mass of rock in the midst of the ice. To be noted are the many indications of movement in the glaciers shown by curved lines, eddies, and crevasses, and the glacial streams flowing away from the ends of the glaciers. The long lobe at the left center shows the formation of both lateral and recessional as well as terminal moraines.

Fig. 43.—A glacial gorge on the northeastern face of Mt. Shasta, California, below Hotlum Glacier (see Fig. 42), the lower end of which is to be seen in the upper part of the photograph. At the left are two ridges, one the edge of a sheet of flow lava, the other, in part at least, a lateral moraine. In the center, at the bottom of the gorge, between the two white lines which represent glacial streams, is a system of concentric ridges which are probably recessional moraines. At the right is the western slope of the gorge. (This figure is the lower overlapping continuation of Fig. 42.)

Fig. 44 Yosemite Valley, California, a typical ice-shaped gorge, showing at the left the granite face of El Capitan, about 3,000 feet above the bottom of the famous gorge, and, at the right, the pinnacle of Sentinel Rock and the well-known form of Half Dome. At the sky line in the center of the picture is Clouds Rest, and well down in the gorge Washington Column and the Royal Arches can be distinguished.

These photographs have the advantage of appealing to the mind through the sense of vision and will serve the same purpose as plaster models. Thus, in Figure 52, a variety of topographic forms are to be distinguished, including slightly dissected highlands with sharply incised gorges; maturely dissected highlands made up now of canyons and ridges; a mountain valley broadening out toward an intermontane plain; several arroyos; and many minor features.

In the interpretation of the features shown in a vertical view of a mountainous country the orientation of the photograph is of prime importance. When viewed in proper orientation, that is, as already pointed out (p. 5), with the shadows falling toward the observer, mountains and valleys appear in their correct relation. But, if the position of the picture is reversed, a mountain will look like a depression and a valley like a ridge. This reversal of the image can be tested by looking at Figures 49 or 52 from both viewpoints. However, since the vertical photographs will be compared with maps of the same area, it is thought better to place them on the page as if they were maps. In order to make them appear natural the prints can be turned in the necessary direction.

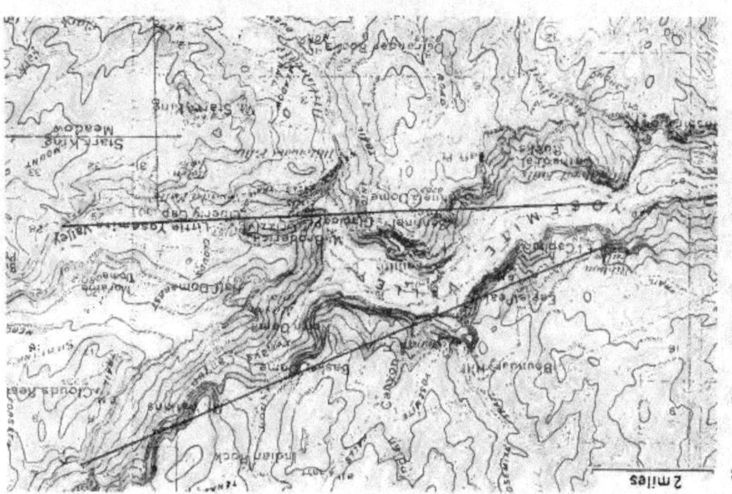

FIG. 45. Map of the Yosemite Valley, showing the area included within the angle of vision of Fig. 44. The map, a reduced section from the Yosemite and Mt. Lyell, Cal., topographic sheets, 1:125,000, published by the U. S. Geological Survey, is oriented for direct comparison with the photograph. Scale, 1:175,000.

FIG. 46.—Mountains of volcanic origin: Cinder Cone with, in the distance at the right, Lassen Peak in the northern Sierra Nevada, California, as seen from an airplane over Lake Bidwell. Beyond, the lake appears the rough surface of lava poured out as molten rock less than two hundred years ago (see *U. S. Geol. Survey Bull. 79*, 1891). Surrounding the cone is a light-colored ash field, sparsely forested at the right, which was formed about two hundred years ago. The mountain in the middle of the photograph having a smooth surface is Cinder Cone, rising 640 feet above the general level of the ash field and consisting of fragments of lava—the so-called ash and cinders—blown from the crater at times of eruption.

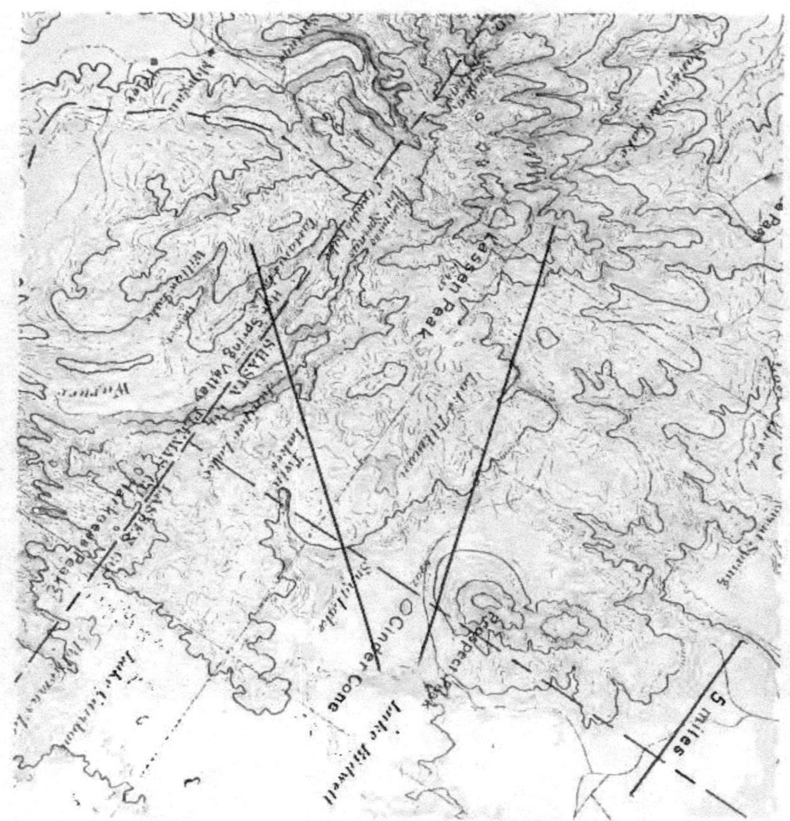

FIG. 47.—Map of the region between Cinder Cone and Lassen Peak in the northern Sierra Nevada, California, showing the area included within the angle of vision of Fig. 46. The map, a reduced section from the Lassen Peak, Cal., topographic sheet, 1:250,000, published by the U. S. Geological Survey, is oriented for direct comparison with the photograph. Scale, 1:307,000.

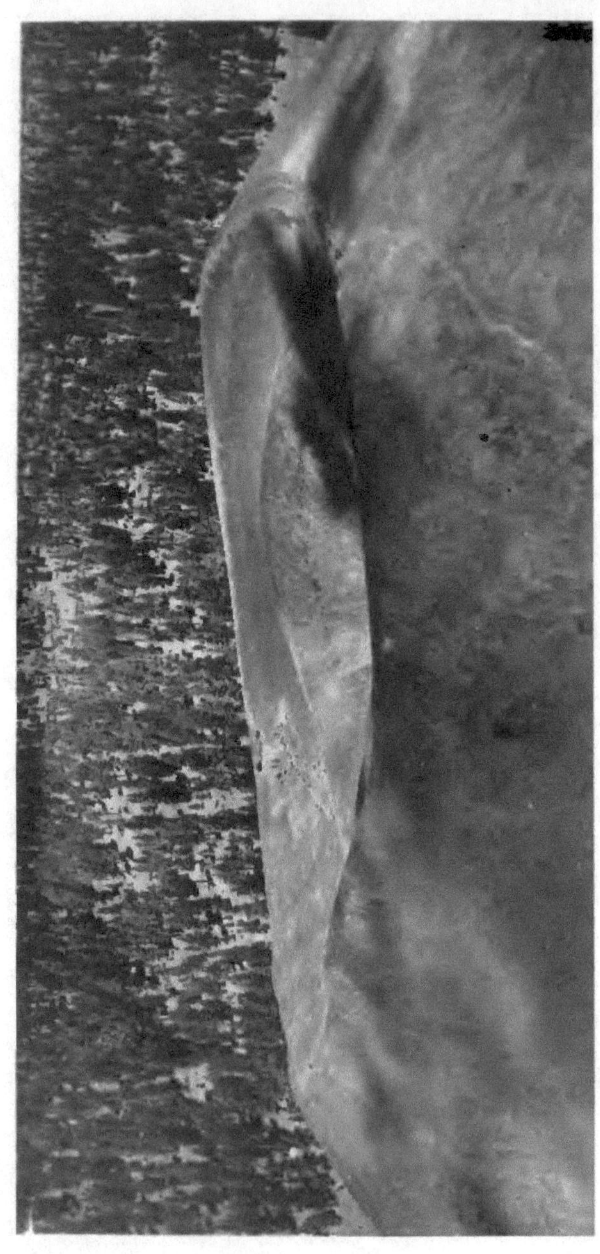

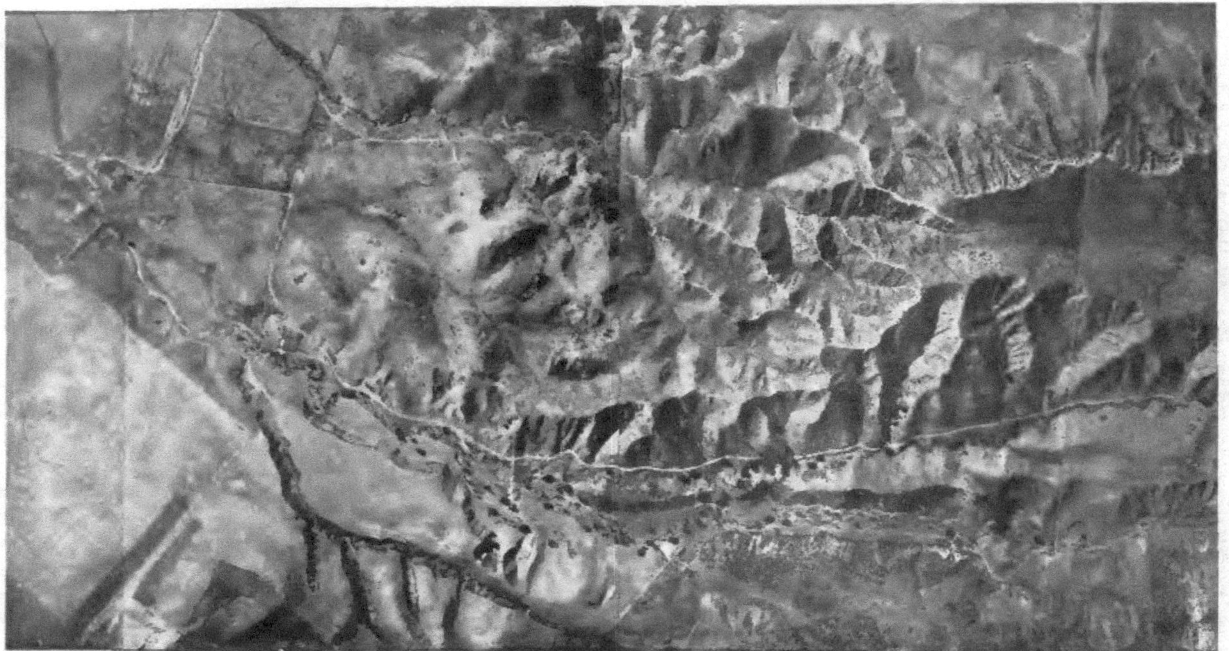

Fig. 49.—Mountain, valley, and plain in the Simi Hills about 15 miles northwest of Santa Monica, Cal. (see Calabasas, Cal., topographic sheet), showing, in the right center of the picture, headward erosion from two parallel valleys, in strong contrast with the gently rounded, slightly dissected part of the mountain (left center) into which the streams have not yet eaten their way. Farther up the mountain is more maturely dissected and the divides are narrow and steep. On its top the mountain shows little effect of stream erosion (right). Strongly cut gorges and arroyos appear where the streams enter the plain (left). Probably north is at the bottom of the photograph. Scale, probably about 1 : 20,000.

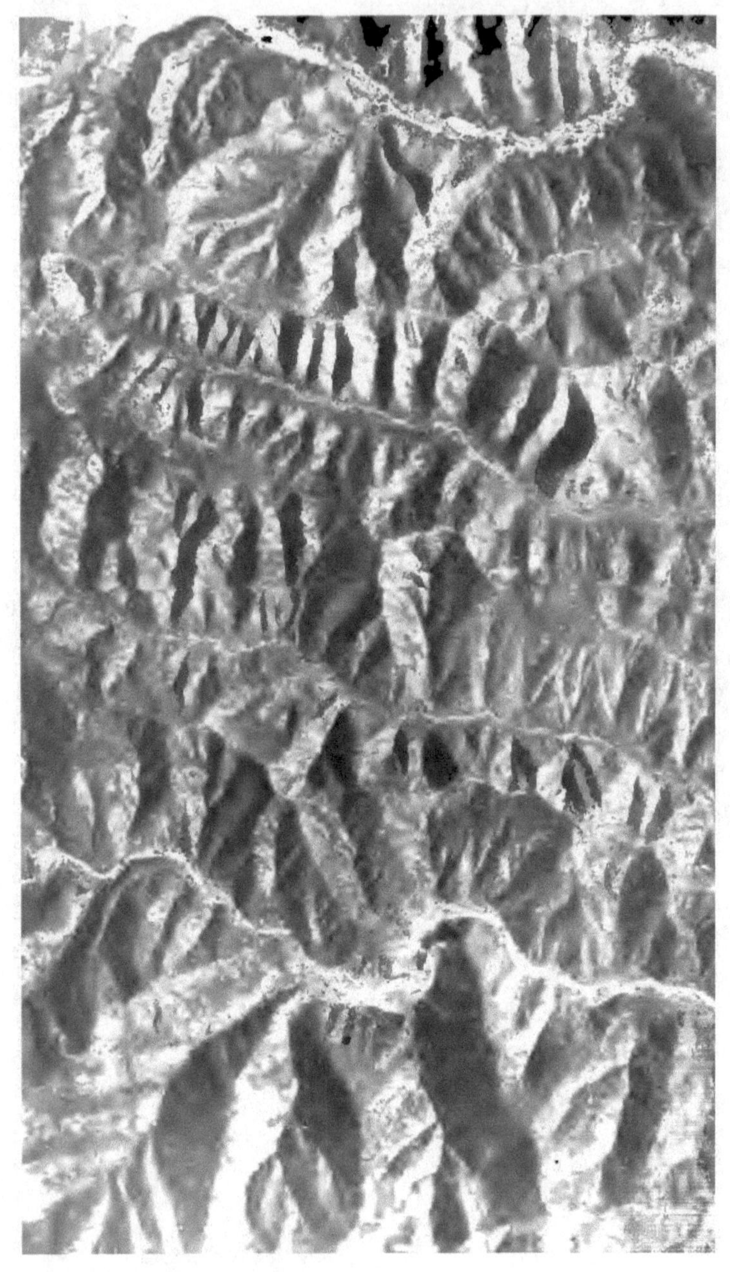

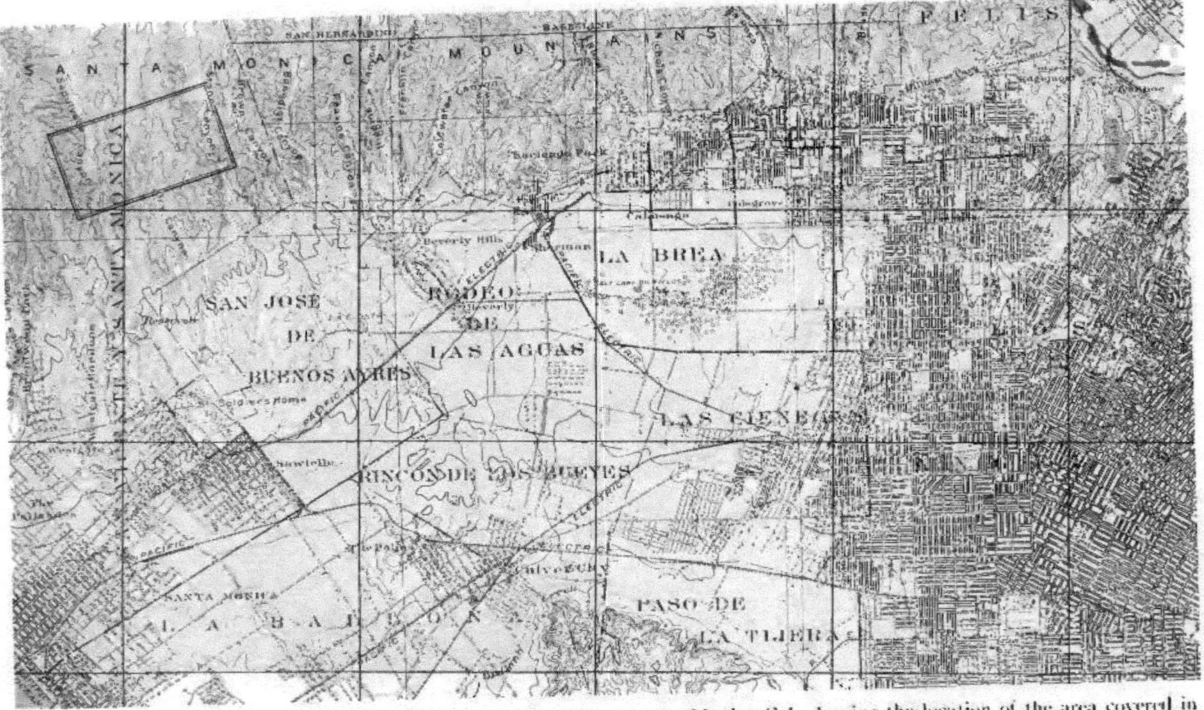

FIG. 51 Map of the region between the center of Los Angeles and Santa Monica, Cal., showing the location of the area covered in Fig. 50 (the double-ruled rectangle in the upper left corner). Reduced from the Santa Monica, Cal., sheet, 1:62,500, of the "Progressive Military Map" of the United States being published by the Corps of Engineers, U.S.A. This sheet, which is the equivalent of the Santa Monica topographic sheet surveyed in 1893 and published by the U.S. Geological Survey, was revised in 1920 by airplane photography. A comparison of the 1893 and 1920 editions brings out strikingly the rapid urban development in this region. Scale, 1:123,000.

Fig. 52 A young mountain gorge showing an erosional hollow developing headward into the less deeply eroded highlands: San Joaquin Hills, a coastal range in Southern California about 45 miles southeast of Los Angeles, near the mouth of Aliso Creek. North is at the left (see Corona, Cal., topographic sheet). Scale, probably about 1 : 10,000.

CHAPTER XI

AIR CRAFT IN THE STUDY OF ROCKS AND ORES

(Fig. 53)

The admirable manner in which air photography lends itself to the observation of geographic relations and physiographic processes suggests its use as a valuable addition to the instruments of geologic reconnaissance; for, not only is the study of geology inseparable from that of physiography, but, in large measure, geology is applied physical geography and many conclusions of a geologic nature are drawn from observed surface relations.

Probably, in most cases, the actual character and composition of rocks cannot be determined from air photographs; but, just as on a good map an area of crystalline rocks can be distinguished from one of sedimentary rocks by means of the topographic expression, so areas of different rocks can be distinguished on photographs. For instance, an area of upturned sedimentary rocks would be readily distinguished from one of horizontal rocks. Figure 42 shows how the character of glaciated mountains is revealed, and Figures 37 to 41 of the Michigan area show well the familiar features of continental glaciation.

It is perhaps premature to say much of the use of the airplane in the study of geology until it has been thoroughly tested. But it should be possible from the air to locate and map ore bodies, metalliferous veins, and outcrops of rock; for it is well known that rocks at the outcrop differ in color, in the forms of erosion developed in them, and in the kind of plants which they support. It is of interest that Colonel Alfred H. Brooks, who was Chief Geologist of the American Expeditionary Forces in France during the war, found that geologic boundaries could be recognized on air photographs and that by means of these photographs he could correct existing geologic maps and iden-

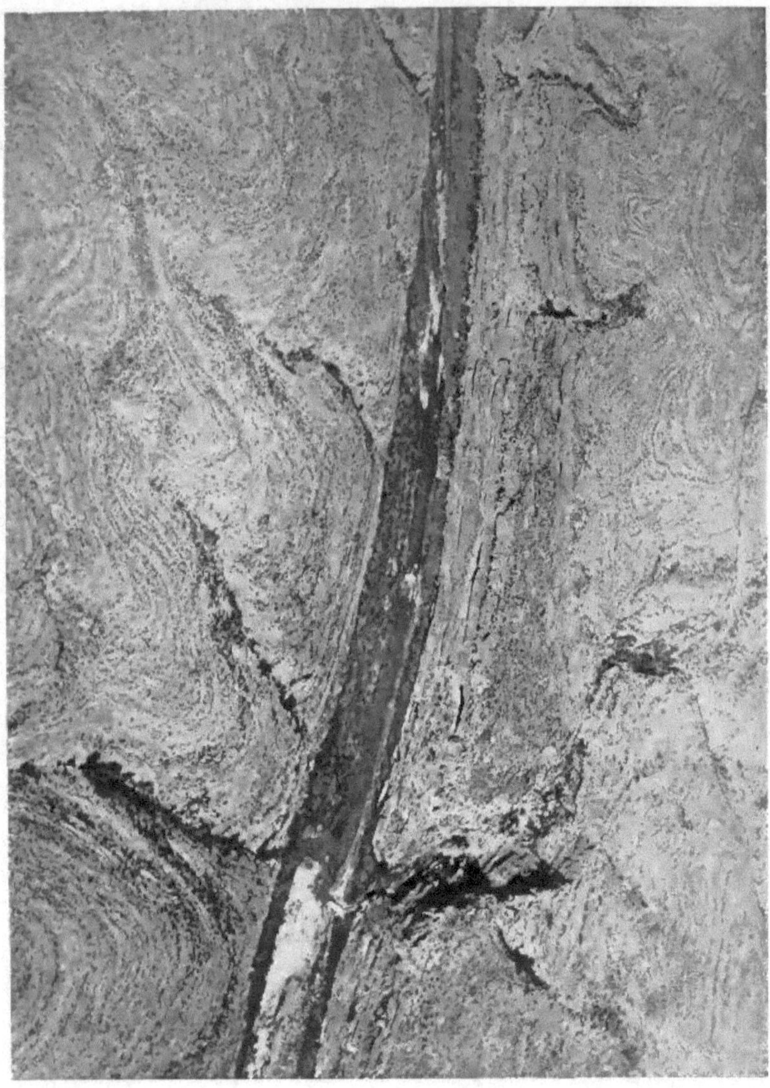

FIG. 53—Canyon in sedimentary rocks near the mouth of the Pecos River, Texas. The rocks consist of flat-lying strata, and the tortuous lines resembling the grain in wood denote the outcrops of hard layers and the benches formed on these layers by erosion. This photograph illustrates the use of air photography in geological reconnaissance. Scale not known.

tify formations in inaccessible areas within the enemy lines. His method was to use air photographs in the study of the geologic formations of areas accessible to him. Then, having familiarized himself with the appearance of the different rock formations and structures on the photographs, he was able to recognize the same features on photographs of areas held by the enemy and so project his mapping over into inaccessible territory.[1]

The prospector should effect a great saving of time by using air photographs to guide him to places where he can find exposures of rock and to help him to avoid places where it would be useless to look for exposures. Particularly in wooded regions air photographs are valuable in indicating localities where exposures can be found in areas so covered with forest that examination on the ground would not be worthy of consideration. Prospectors for oil are planning to use airplanes for this purpose in northern Canada, in South America, and in other places where much of the country is so densely wooded that much time is usually spent in looking for clear space.

Use in Exploration

Exploratory work should benefit in many ways. General reconnaissance has been carried on to a considerable extent in foreign lands with airplanes and to some extent also in America. Wide areas along the Mexican border have been photographed for the making of new maps and for the correction of existing maps. The same photographs would be useful in geologic reconnaissance. The new photographs of southern Arizona are said to show mountain ranges many miles away from their location on existing maps. Such corrections are of importance to the geologist as well as to the geographer and the map-maker. Amundsen intends to employ several small planes in his Arctic work now under way. Mjöberg[2] has projected an expedition to New Guinea in which the use of airplanes is a fundamental condition.

[1] A. H. Brooks, personal communication.

[2] Eric Mjöberg: A Proposed Aërial Expedition for the Exploration of the Unknown Interior of New Guinea, *Geogr. Rev.*, Vol. 3, 1917, pp. 89-106.

CHAPTER XII

MAPPING AND CHARTING FROM THE AIR

(FIGS. 54 TO 82)

Mention has already been made (p. 56) of the experiment in map-making carried out by the Army Air Service and the United States Geological Survey at Schoolcraft, Mich. The results of that experiment and of others of the sort are sufficient to establish the fact that the air camera is destined to become a valuable addition to the map-maker's equipment. The extent to which it will be used depends, of course, upon the degree to which its present imperfections are corrected and its possibilities developed. The Board of Surveys and Maps of the United States government has recently published the results of its study of air photography for use in map-making.[1]

[1] The Use of Aerial Photographs in Topographic Mapping: A Report of the Committee on Photographic Surveying of the Board of Surveys and Maps of the Federal Government, 1920, *Air Service Information Circular (Aviation) No. 184*, War Department, Washington, D. C., 1921.

FIG. 54—View across the western end of Lake Erie, looking in a northeasterly direction (see Fig. 55). Oblique photograph taken from 18,000 feet above Port Clinton, Ohio, by Lieut. G. W. Goddard, showing, in the foreground at the right, Catawba "Island," a part of the mainland, and, at the left, Put-in-Bay and the islands around it. In the distance below the white clouds are a small island (Middle Island) and a large one (Pelee Island). In the upper left-hand corner is seen Point Pelee and the Canadian shore to the northeast of it about 30 miles away. At Put-in-Bay was fought, September 10, 1813, the Battle of Lake Erie, in which Commodore Perry defeated the British. The monument commemorating this victory can be distinguished in the photograph as a white shaft.

Although most vertical airplane photographs are in the nature of large-scale maps, this view illustrates how a large area can be covered in an oblique view taken at a high altitude—an area, when transformed, of appreciable size even on a small-scale map, such as, for example, Fig. 55.

FIG. 55—Map of the western end of Lake Erie showing the area covered within the angle of vision of Fig. 54. Scale, 1: 1,400,000.

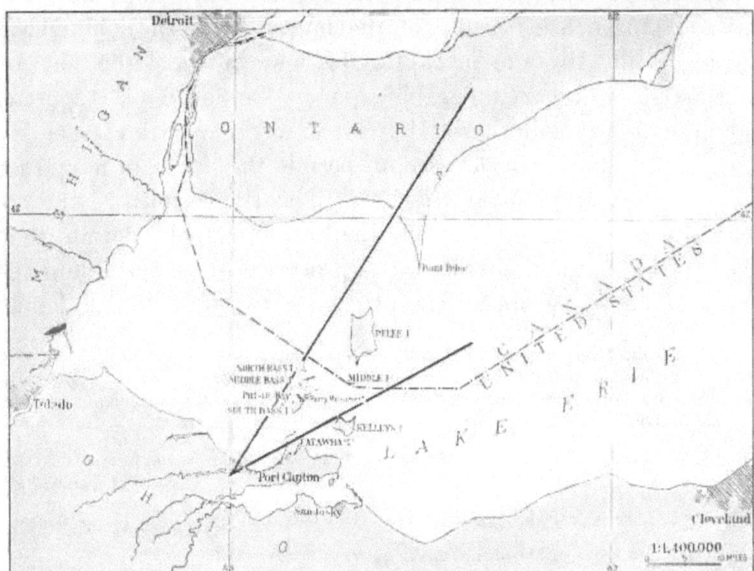

FIGS. 54 (upper) and 55 (lower). For explanation, see bottom of opposite page.

Scale and Horizontal Control of Vertical Photographs

The vertical photographs taken with an air camera are, of course, of the order of large-scale maps.[2] For a lens of 6-inch focus the scale at an elevation of 2,500 feet will be 1:5,000; at 5,000 feet, 1:10,000; and at 10,000 feet, 1:20,000.[3] Air mapping, therefore, lends itself best to the production of such maps as engineering maps, city plans, topographic maps, and coast charts. In all of these maps a degree of accuracy is demanded that will give the exact location of all the features included on the map and permit the precise measurement of distances between them. To obtain such accuracy necessitates an elaborate system of control stations as a basis on which the surveyor works out his triangulations and traverses. In the United States these controls have been established principally by the United States Coast and Geodetic Survey.[4] To construct a map from air photographs, varying in scale and distorted as they often are because of the impossibility of holding the plane at an absolute level and because of the stretching or shrinkage of the photographic paper, would require a great amount of triangulation and traverse in order that the control might be sufficiently detailed to permit the accurate mounting of the photographic prints. But, given these controls, the air camera can, without further adaptation, supply details that heretofore required the laborious processes of plane-table mapping. The topographer can place the two-dimensional details

[2] What can be done, however, by photographing obliquely from a high altitude, thereby increasing the area in the field of vision, is illustrated by Figure 54, which encompasses Lake Erie from one shore to the other and, in its representation of the main features of the region, is akin to maps on a relatively small scale, such as 1:1,000,000.

[3] J. W. Bagley: The Use of the Panoramic Camera in Topographic Surveying, With Notes on the Application of Photogrammetry to Aerial Surveys, *U. S. Geol. Survey Bull. 657*, p. 84. "The scale of the photograph is given by the relation $\frac{f}{H}$, f being the focal length of the lens and H the height of the camera above ground." (*Ibid.*)

[4] E. Lester Jones: The Aeroplane in Surveying and Mapping, *Flying*, June, 1919, pp. 438–441, 472, and 476.

ROCHESTER

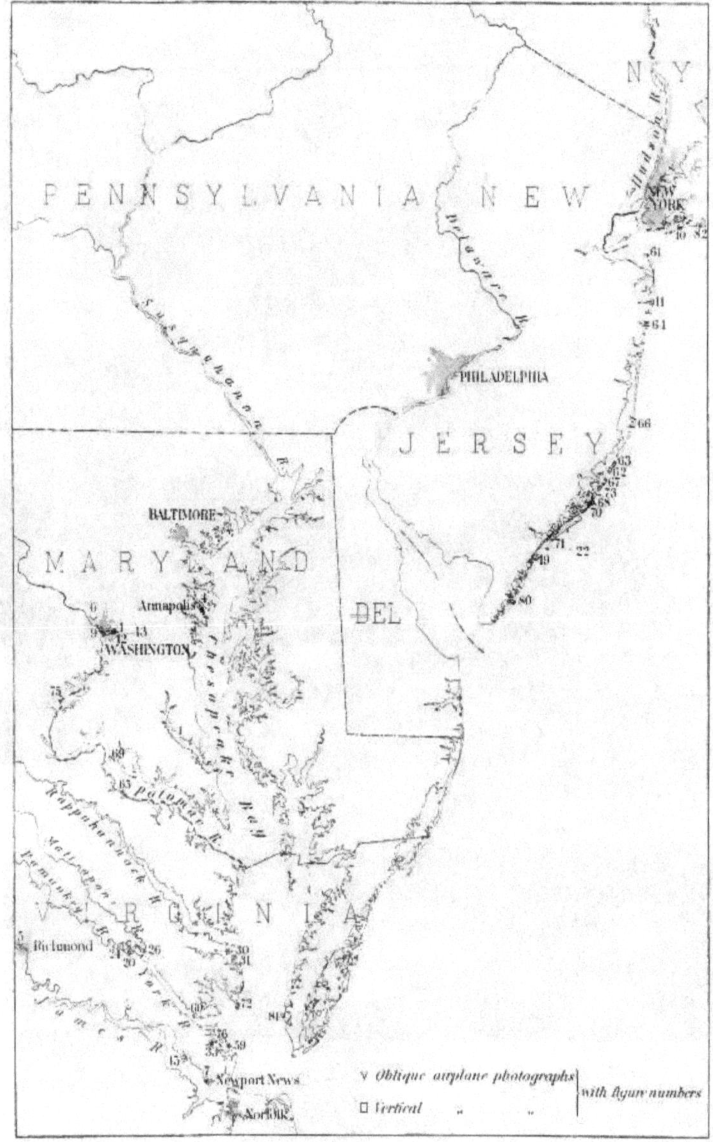

FIG. 58 Index map showing the location of the areas shown on airplane photographs in this book within the Atlantic seaboard of the northeastern United States, except those whose exact location is unknown (Figs. 21, 23, 28, 29, and 77). Scale. 1 : 2,800,000.

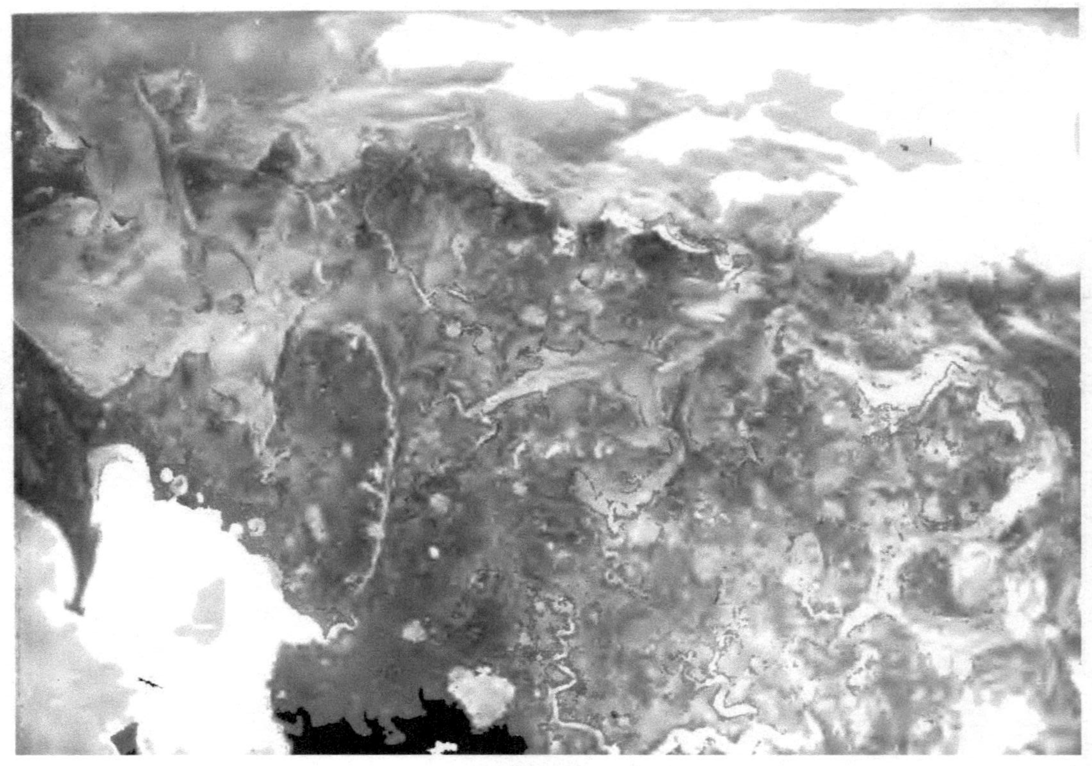

FIG. 59 An area where charting of the coast line is difficult. Marshlands on Chesapeake Bay which are exposed at low tide and submerged at high tide. Location: South of the mouth of the York River, Virginia, between the estuaries of Poquoson River and Back River. Scale, about 1: 2,500.

from photographs and then go into the field with only the contouring to be done.

USE IN CITY MAPPING

In city mapping, even though time be taken to establish a very elaborate system of controls, the air camera can accomplish in a few hours a task of years by ordinary methods. In fact it is only by means of air photographs that maps of a growing city can be kept at all up to date. Paris was mapped with 800 plates in less than one day of actual flying. Washington was completely mapped in two and a half hours with less than 200 exposures.[5] For the mosaic of Rochester, N. Y. (Fig. 56) 82 photographs were made in one hour and twenty minutes. There is no reason why such a mosaic with an original survey or even a number of accurately located points as a basis of control should not be sufficiently accurate for all purposes.

USE IN REVISION OF EXISTING MAPS

Another immediate use of air photographs in mapping is in the correction and revision of existing maps. So far as individual features are concerned, the air photograph is an exact record of the area exposed to its lens, and natural and artificial features are easily transferred from the picture to the map. Its great value in the saving of time and money has been demonstrated in the rapidly developing territory near Los Angeles. In 1893 the Santa Monica quadrangle was surveyed, and houses, roads, etc., as they existed at that time, are shown on the map. This area was later built up and so changed that the map was practically worthless. From information derived from air photographs the map was revised in 1920 (Fig. 51). Evidence has already been given of the efficiency of the air photograph in elaborating maps where the importance of the region is not sufficient to warrant the expense of a detailed survey of minor features, and in mapping areas inaccessible from the ground.

[5] H. E. Ives: Airplane Photography, 1920, pp. 407–408.

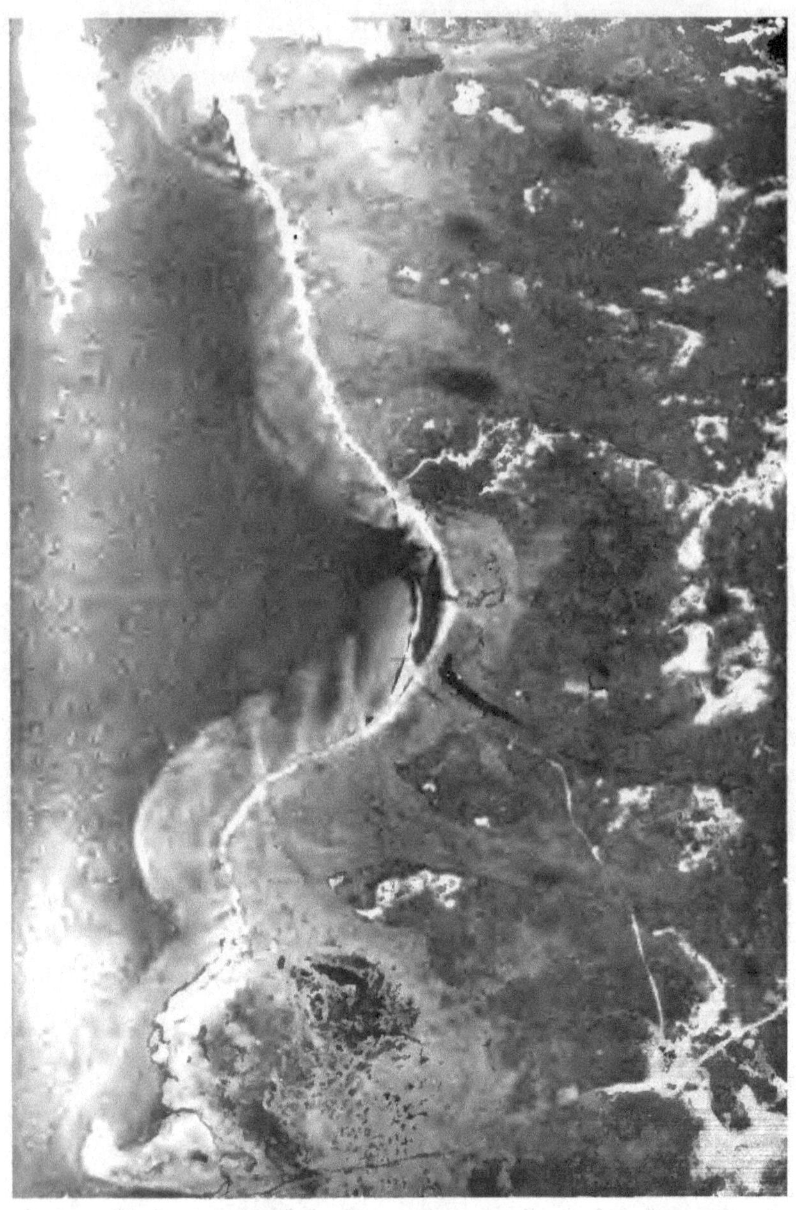

FIG. 62– Beach cusps extended under water and showing the interference of waves off the curved beach on the bay side north of Beach Haven, N. J. Scale, about 1: 3,000.

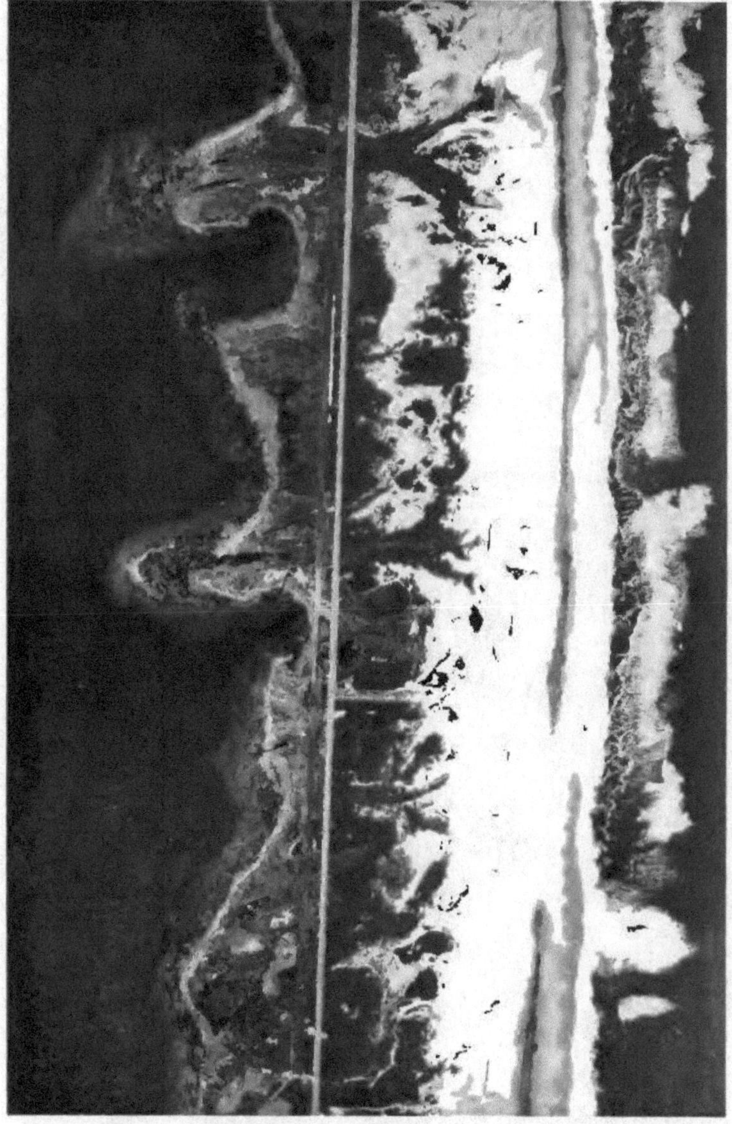

FIG. 63 First stage in the formation of an inlet through a barrier beach, where ocean waves during some storm, probably at high tide, broke over the sand barrier 2 miles north of Beach Haven, N. J., and washed some of its sand into Little Egg Harbor. (For another good example of wash-overs, see Fig. 68.) Scale, about 1:9,000.

FIG. 64—A tidal delta in Shark River Inlet, Belmar, N. J., as photographed from a height of 10,000 feet, showing shoals at the left, which appear shadowy because they are under water, and the small channels which radiate outward from the narrow inlet like the ribs of a fan. They are the distributaries of this underwater delta. Scale, about 1:11,000.

It is fortunate for those engaged in the study of shore features and the mapping of coasts that, being flat, shore features are particularly well adapted to representation by air photographs, for on coasts exposed to the wind and waves the channels, shoals and bars are continually changing. Air photography offers a

FIG. 65 —A tidal delta built up until it is partly above water: Popes Creek, Virginia, on the right bank of the lower Potomac River, 4 miles southeast of Colonial Beach, as seen obliquely from a height of 4 000 feet at 3:30 P. M., August 31, 1920. The tidal currents from the Potomac have built hook-shaped bars nearly across the outlet of the creek, and the inflowing currents have built a delta from the mouth of the creek upstream.

quick and convenient means of keeping charts up to date. The intricacies of the water line in some places makes accurate charting by the ordinary survey methods a slow, laborious process. When bluffs or relatively steep slopes, like those of York River, Virginia, near Gloucester Point, shown in Figure 60,

FIG. 66. (For explanation, see next page.)

FIG. 66—A double tidal delta at Barnegat Inlet, New Jersey, as photographed from a height of 10,000 feet. To the east (right) the breaking waves and shadowy depths indicate the position of shoals. West of the surf belt are the light-colored beach sand, shading off from the conspicuous hook at the southern end of Island Beach into underwater shoals and bars, and older surfaces made dark-colored by the growth of plants. South of the hook are the inlet leading into Barnegat Bay and the northern end of Long Beach, at the point of which stands a lighthouse whose long shadow is to be seen across the beach sand. The mottled appearance of the bay to the left is due to shoals slightly submerged or perhaps exposed at low tide, where dark-colored drainage lines appear, and shading off to deeper water, where the submerged land forms have a shadowy appearance. The distribution of the shoals indicates that this is a double tidal delta, an in-facing part west of the inlet and an ocean-facing part to the right. Scale, about 1:17,000.

FIG. 67—A tidal inlet through the barrier beach south of Beach Haven, N. J., connecting the Atlantic Ocean to the right (east) with Little Egg Harbor to the left. The beach sand south of the inlet is little above water level and is frequently washed by waves, which shift the sand and produce the clouded appearance of the sandy surface. The light-colored ragged belt at the right is surf; the continuous narrow belt, beach sand; the clouded areas, recently washed wet or slightly submerged sand. (The ordinary tidal variation here is 4.2 feet.) This inlet does not appear on the 1914 edition of U. S. Coast and Geodetic Survey Chart 1216, and sand hooks had little more than begun to form then. Scale, about 1:14,000.

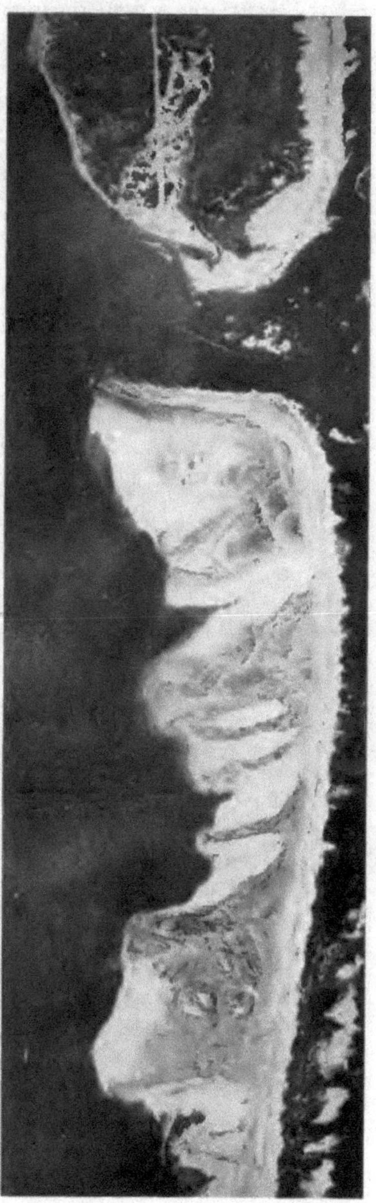

FIG. 67

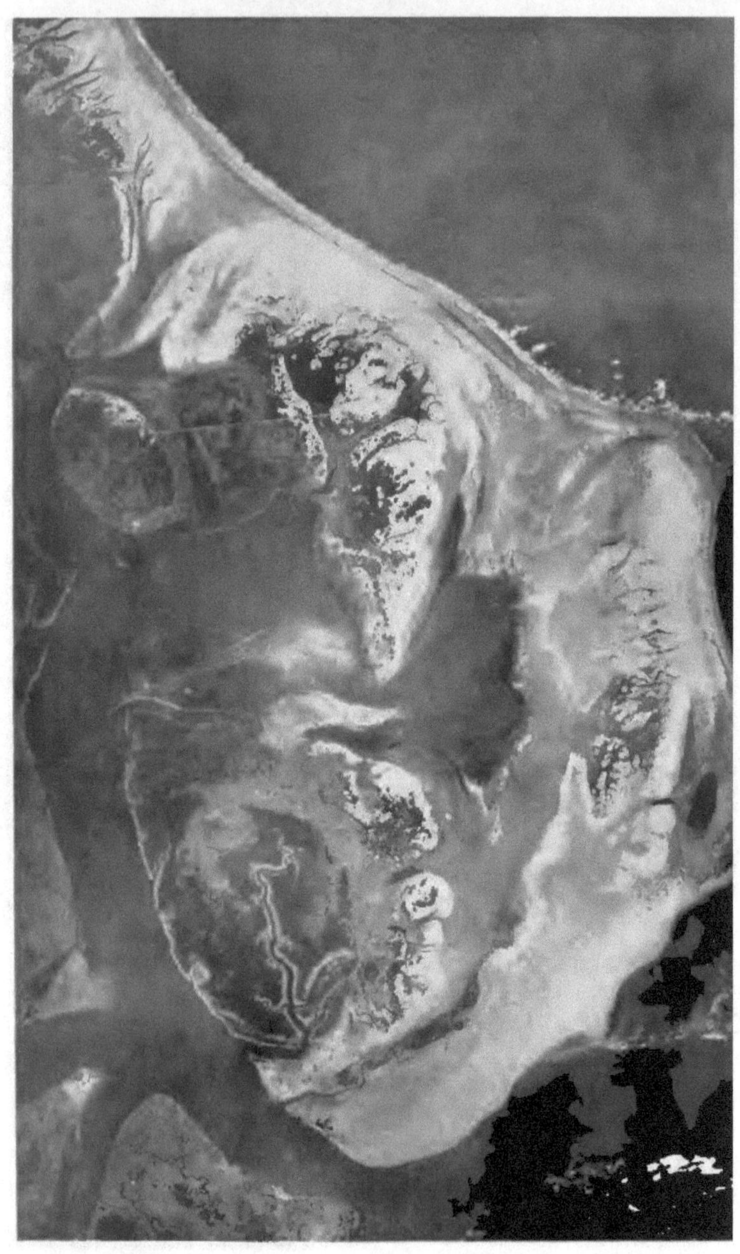

FIG. 68. (For explanation see bottom of next page.)

occur along the shore, the water line varies little from year to year. But on very low lands, like those along Chesapeake Bay south of the mouth of York River, shown in Figure 59, the strand may migrate over a broad belt between high and low tide. For this reason it is desirable that photographs of areas affected by the tide be accompanied by a record of the date and time of day at which the exposure was made, in order that the

FIG. 69—A simple spit: Lower Cedar Point, Maryland, on the left bank of the lower Potomac River, 6 miles north of Colonial Beach, Va., as seen obliquely downward from a height of 4,000 feet. The white line on either side of the point is sand at the foot of bluffs. Houses and fields are seen at the left.

height of the tide at the time of exposure can be computed. As the shore on the Coast and Geodetic Survey charts denotes the water line at high tide, a photograph taken at low tide might be interpreted as indicating an error on the chart. Where the water migrates over such a broad belt of sand or mud, the prob-

FIG. 68—Beach between Brigantine and Little Egg Inlets, New Jersey, showing a variety of features characteristic of a wave-built sand barrier. The upper (northern) part of the illustration shows several places where waves have broken over the sand barrier and washed the sand westward, where it was redeposited at the left in the quiet, protected water. Farther south are older wash-overs, where the enclosed bay is nearly filled with sand. At the left are numerous islands, streams, and flats characteristic of the salt marshes west of the barrier beach along the New Jersey coast. Scale, about 1 : 7,000.

lems of charting become very troublesome. Photographs of such areas could be taken at both low and high tide, and from these the belt of daily flooding could be charted.

FIG. 70—A hook, or recurved spit, south of Brigantine Inlet, New Jersey, as photographed from a height of 10,000 feet, showing the strong curving upstream characteristic of spits on this ocean-facing coast. The growing end of the spit, resembling a lily bud, shows an underwater extension beyond the light-colored beach sand. To be noted is the filling in of the lagoon behind the reef and its pools and drainage lines. This figure is practically a southern continuation of Fig. 68. Scale, about 1:9,000.

EXPERIMENTS BY THE UNITED STATES, FRENCH, AND OTHER COAST SURVEYS

The use of photographs in charting the coast line was tested by the United States Coast and Geodetic Survey.[6] A flight was

[6] E. Lester Jones: Surveying From the Air, *Science*, Vol. 52, 1920 (Oct. 17), pp. 574-575, and *Engineering News-Record*, Dec. 16, 1920, pp. 1184-1186.

made over the coast of New Jersey by Captain A. W. Stevens of the United States Army Air Service, March 20, 1920, in a plane equipped with a K-1 camera of 10-inch focal length, which makes negatives 18 by 24 centimeters in size. During the flight the camera was maintained at an altitude of about 10,000 feet. The course was covered by 183 exposures made at such

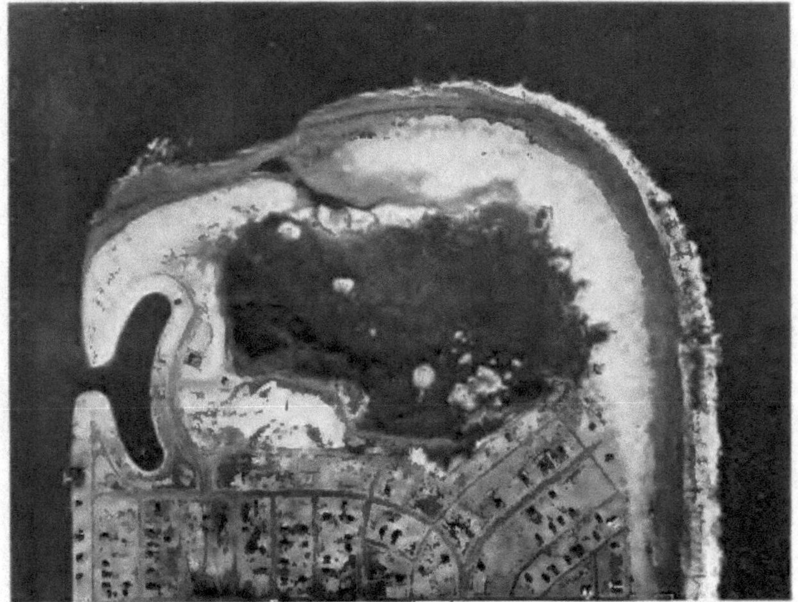

FIG. 71—A hook, or recurved spit, showing interference with natural growth: The northern end of Ocean City, N. J., as photographed from a height of 10,000 feet. At the right (east) appears the curved body of sand, light-colored where dried, darker-colored where bathed by the waves and fringed by surf. To the left certain "improvements" seem to have interfered with the natural growth of the spit, and a small bay of shallow water has been enclosed by the formation of a bay-mouth bar across the outlet to the north. Scale, about 1: 14,000.

intervals of time that the prints overlap. Unfortunately the exposures were not sufficient to give all the details desired for marsh and water areas, but prints were made on developing paper suitable for showing extreme contrast. These were matched together and a continuous picture obtained. A part

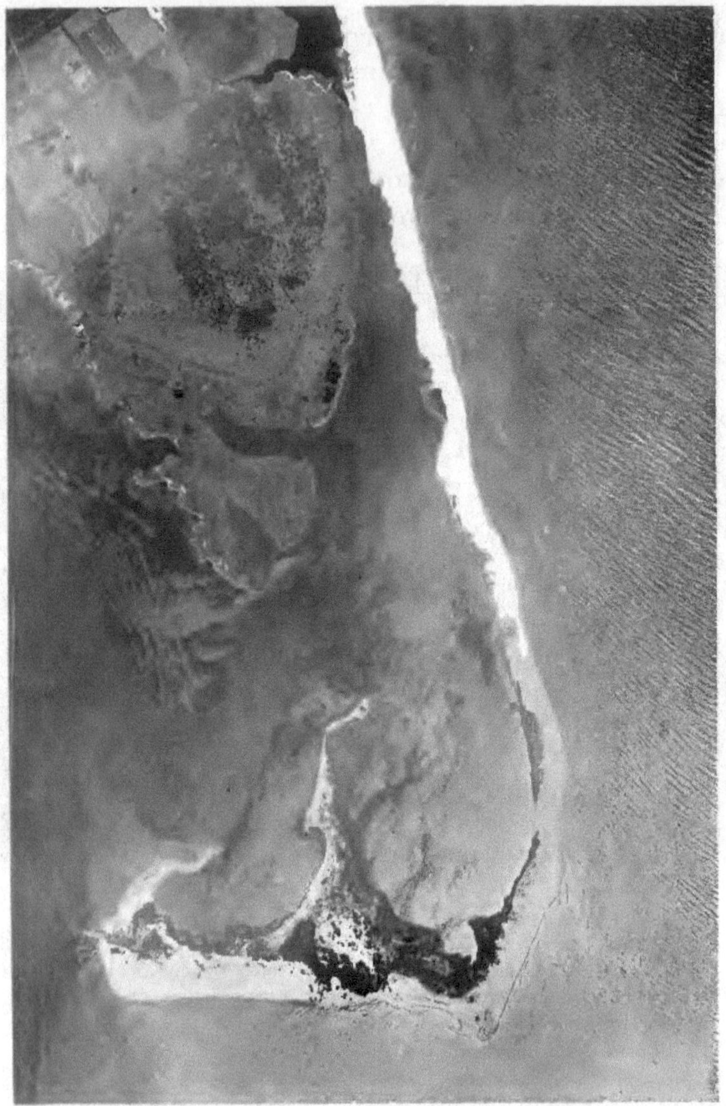

FIG. 72—New Point Comfort, a complex recurved spit at the tip of the peninsula enclosed by the York and Rappahannock Rivers, Virginia. A vertical view taken from an altitude of about 10,000 feet, showing in order from right to left (east to west): the wavy surface of Chesapeake Bay; a light-colored band of beach sand curving westward in a compound hook made dark-colored in some places by trees and brush; a shallow bay west of the beach in which may be seen shoals, channels, and sand bars under water; and low-lying areas showing woodland and cultivated fields. The photograph was taken at a time of day when reflected light from the partly enclosed body of water was dispersed, allowing the submerged forms to appear. Scale, about 1 : 12,000.

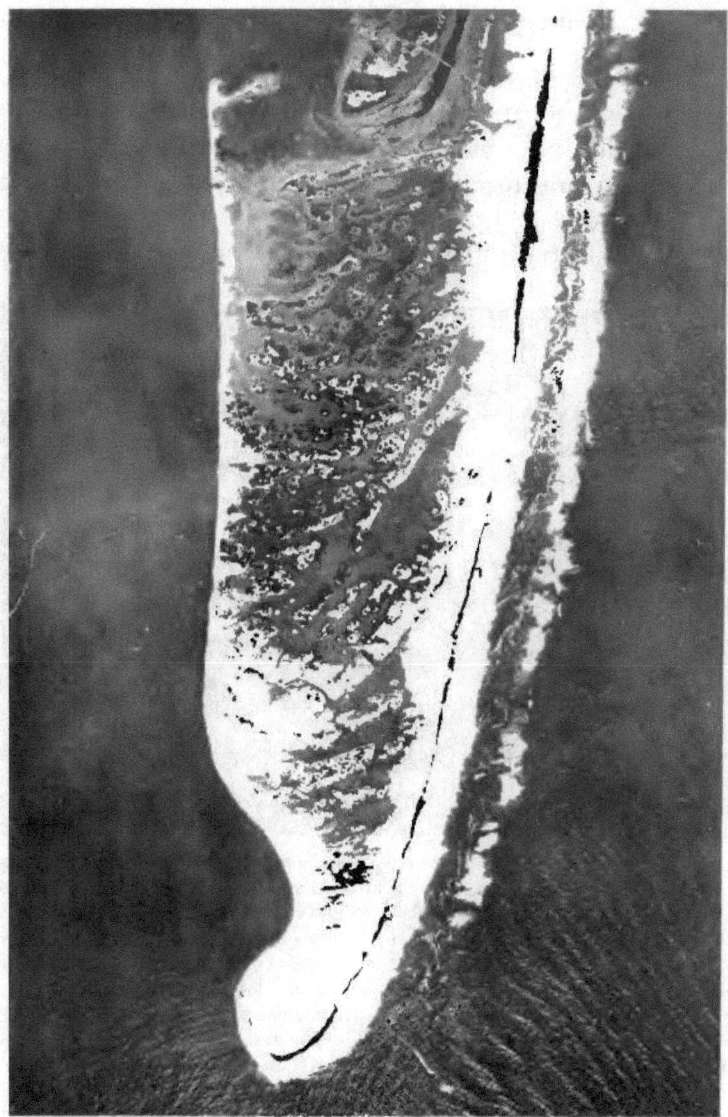

FIG. 73.—Lines of growth in a sand spit: Tucker Beach, New Jersey, as photographed from a height of 10,000 feet, showing the growth southward by successive ridges, which probably began as sand bars, grew to be barriers by wave action, were heightened by wind-blown sand, and finally were added to the main body of the spit by the final filling of the enclosed lagoons. To the right (east) is the Atlantic Ocean, showing waves and surf near the light-colored beach sand. Farther to the left are the ridges of sand made dark-colored by vegetation, bordered by light-colored beach sand on Little Egg Inlet, which appears to the south and west. Scale, about 1: 14,000.

of this picture, greatly reduced, is reproduced as Figure 22. Several characteristic shore and salt marsh features are illustrated by this series of photographs, and these are reproduced in separate figures together with illustrations of special features in other places.

The main features illustrated in detail, all of which are con-

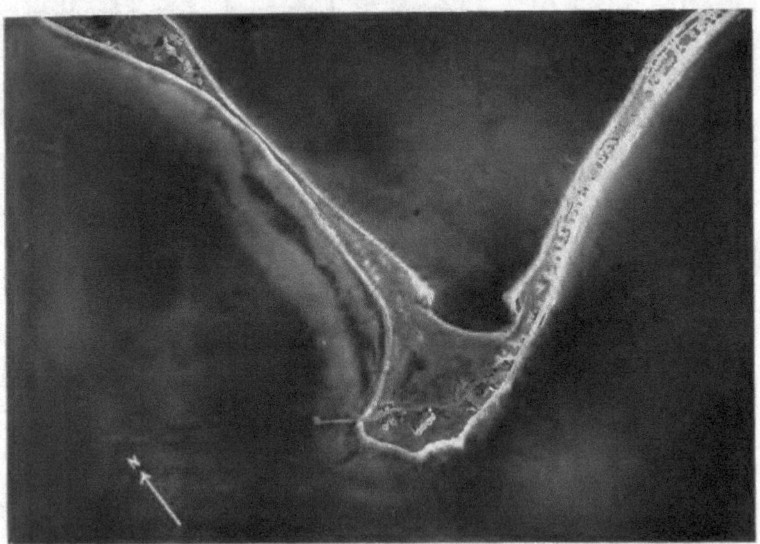

FIG. 74 An island developing toward the stage of being tied to the mainland by a double tombolo, or connecting bar: Napatree Point, as photographed from a height of about 10,000 feet, connected to the east by Napatree Beach with the mainland at Watch Hill, R. I., and approaching connection to the north with the mainland near Stonington, Conn. On the outer side of the tombolos underwater shoals and bars are seen dimly at the right (south, Block Island Sound side) and more clearly at the left (west, Fishers Island Sound), where the boat landing is situated at the edge of a submerged shelf. The surf appears as a thin white line, the beach sand as a narrow light-colored belt, and the higher land as dark-colored areas on which houses and other structures stand. Scale, about 1:24,000.

tinually liable to change, making the keeping of a map of the area at all up to date impossible by ordinary means, are as follows: coast of low-lying mainland (Fig. 60); mud or peat-covered beach (Fig. 59); sandy beach (Fig. 63); barrier beach (Fig. 67);

beach cusps (Figs. 61 and 62); recurved spits or sand hooks (Fig. 70 and others); compound hook (Fig. 72); lines of growth in the development of hooks (Figs. 73): tombolos and tied islands (Figs. 60 and 74).

Another experiment was made by the Coast and Geodetic Survey off the coast of Florida, where the water is clear, in an

FIG. 75—Oblique view of the mouth of Powells Creek, Virginia, on the right bank of the lower Potomac River, 5 miles west of the Naval Proving Grounds at Indian Head, showing at the left the inner channel winding through the slightly submerged shoals and fading out toward the right where the channel crosses the submerged terrace of the Potomac.

attempt to photograph "the small coral heads and pinnacle rocks" which may be disastrous to boats. The report states that the results were unsatisfactory and concludes that airplane pictures are useful in "aerial photo-topography" but not in

FIG. 76 Channels, shoals, and terraces in a drowned river valley: Roberts Creek, 9 miles southeast of Yorktown, Va., an estuary tributary to Chesapeake Bay. Under the water in the drowned valley is seen the channel, "braided" in some places, and extending out through sand bars to the deep water of Poquoson River shown at the top (north) of the illustration. At the left the dark-colored forest area is fringed with a narrow strip of white beach sand, then with a belt of shallow water at the outer edge of which the waves form an irregular white line, and beyond this with a belt which represents a submerged terrace. Scale, about 1 : 14,000.

FIG. 77.—The underwater channel in Quantico Bay. Quantico Creek is a tributary of the Potomac River entering from the Virginia side, about 28 miles downstream from Washington. The "Bay" is the widened part of the stream at its entrance into the Potomac, which is entered by the tide. Forested land appears at the right and left, with light-colored fields at the left. The space between the wooded areas is occupied by shallow water, beneath which appears the relatively deep channel, which forks after the manner of streams. The branching channel is wholly under water and differs in some respects from the channel of a normal stream. Among the more obvious peculiarities is the "fanning out" of the headwaters. Photograph taken from a height of about 18,000 feet. Scale, about 1:21,000.

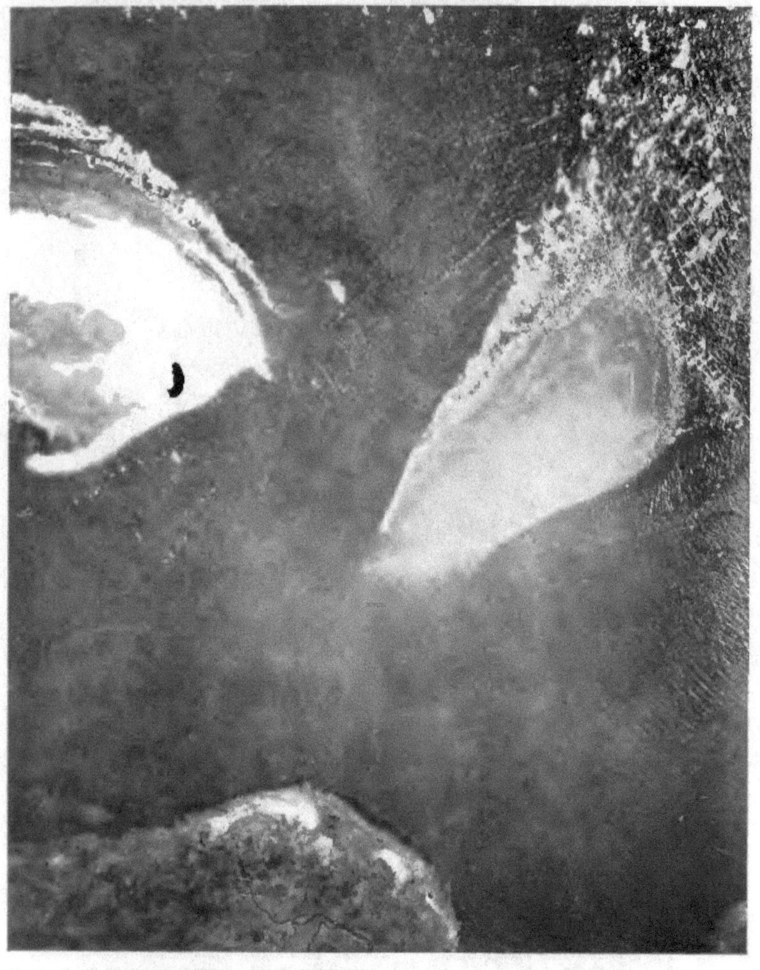

Fig. 80 A shoal in Hereford Inlet north of Wildwood, N. J., as seen from a height of 10,000 feet. The breaking waves indicate that the shoal is only slightly submerged. (Tidal variation is here about 4 feet.) The sand spit north of the shoal, the south end of Sevenmile Beach, like other spits of the New Jersey coast, is building southward and may in time annex the shoal. Scale, about 1:13,000.

FIG. 81—Sand bars at Cape Charles, Va. South of the town at the right is the harbor, into which a tug-boat is towing a barge. West of the town (left) is a belt of light-colored beach sand and sand bars ending at the south against the breakwater, north of the harbor. The sand bars appear somewhat dim because they were photographed through water. They are under water 1 to 6 feet deep at low tide, or 4 to 9 feet at high tide. Scale, about 1:6,000.

"aerial photo-hydrography."[7] On the other hand, Volmat reports the successful use of air photography for similar purposes on the French coast, where photographs of objects down to a depth of 17 meters (about 56 feet) were found useful in several ways—among others, the discovery of points of rock which had

[7] E. Lester Jones, *op. cit.* (*Science*), p. 575.

FIG. 82.—Bars, channels, beaches, and marsh near Far Rockaway, Long Island, N. Y., as photographed from a height of 7,000 feet at 11 A. M., September 15, 1920. In order from the bottom of the picture upward are: East Rockaway Inlet with a shoal to the left and the sand hook at the end of Long Beach to the right of it; the beach south of Far Rockaway with streets and houses; a group of boats in the inlet at the right of the beach; an area of salt marsh that is filling the lagoon behind the barrier beach; and a small section of the village of Far Rockaway. Scale, about 1:12,000.

escaped attention during very detailed surveys. He states that with proper plates and ray filters the presence of objects invisible to the eye is revealed by the camera.[8] Similar use of air photographs has been made by the English in charting reefs, shallows, and harbors. Thomas says: "In 1917 aeroplane photography was successfully used for charting the harbor of Rahbeg on the Arabian coast."[9] It is a well-known fact that, under proper conditions, objects submerged to a considerable depth under clear water can be seen from points high above the surface. During the war, submarines were detected and followed by observers in airplanes, and sunken vessels, mines, and other submerged objects have been located by observation from the air. Illustrations in this paper show the possibility of using this method of observation, to some extent at least, in detecting and mapping shoals, channels, and other features under water.

Photographs of channels like those of the Potomac River and its tributaries will be commercially as well as scientifically valuable. The deep-water channel of the Potomac is well known and has been charted; but very little is known of many of the small tributary channels, such as that of Powells Creek (Fig. 75). Where the channels are not well known, such a photograph could be used to advantage in avoiding the shoals, and, by surveyors, first in exploratory work and later as a general guide in charting. Small boats entering this channel could use the photographs either for the original location of the deep channel in case no chart were available or for detecting changes in its course after the chart was made. For uncharted channels, like those of many of the tributaries of the Potomac River, air

[8] J. Volmat: Application de la photographie aérienne aux levés hydrographiques, *Comptes Rendus de l'Acad. des Sci. [de Paris]*, Vol. 169, 1919, Oct. 27, pp. 717–718; *idem:* Rapport sur la mission photohydrographique de Brest (1919), *Annales Hydrogr.* (publ. by Service Hydrographique de la Marine, Paris), 3rd Series, 1919–20, pp. 191–220, with seven air photographs and corresponding sections from French coast charts.

[9] H. Hamshaw Thomas: Geographical Reconnaissance by Aeroplane Photography, With Special Reference to the Work Done on the Palestine Front, *Geogr. Journ.*, Vol. 55, 1920, pp. 349–376; reference on p. 369.

photography furnishes a quick and accurate means of location.

No amount of sounding, charting, or description could produce so accurate a mental picture of a drowned valley as that produced by Figure 76. In Figures 78 and 79, both of which were taken near Miami, Florida, is illustrated the difference in appearance between natural and artificial channels. The straightaway course and regular outlines of the dredged channel contrast sharply with the winding course and merging outlines of the natural channel. To the student of physiography and earth history the photographs furnish a means of observation of a definiteness heretofore quite unthought-of. On them the actual shape of the channels, submerged terraces, and drowned land forms are shown in detail.

Improvements Under Way Point to Promising Outlook for Airplane Photography

There is, however, need of careful research to determine the conditions under which the best results can be obtained. The height and time of day for exposures with a certain lens, the emulsion and kind of ray filter best suited under certain conditions, the effect of light as it enters and emerges from the water, and the effect of polarization are subjects demanding consideration. Chief among the experiments now under way is the determination of the kind of emulsion and ray filter or color screen that will give the best results. It is a demonstrated fact that, with an emulsion sensitive to red light, objects in the air invisible to the eye because of intervening haze can be photographed through a red filter. It is possible that water can be penetrated in the same way and that filters of other colors will prove advantageous.

Certainly, the air photograph is only in its infancy—but an infancy full of promise. As a means of securing new and advantageous views of subjects of interest, it is not only entertaining but scientifically and commercially valuable. As an aid in mapping it can, even in its present stage of development, serve an important purpose by supplying accurate knowledge of otherwise inaccessible regions, by furnishing details that are valuable but expensive to obtain, and by permitting the frequent and inexpensive revision of existing maps.

INDEX

Zeitfracht Medien GmbH
Ferdinand-Jühlke-Straße 7
99095 Erfurt, Deutschland
produktsicherheit@kolibri360.de